Carrying his father's medical bag, Doc walked out of the house and came to a stop on the porch. Silence fell over the grim-faced crowd who were hovering in front of the building and guarding the two hostages. They realized that the operation had come to an end and waited to be told its result. "I've taken out the piece of bone and relieved the pressure on his brain like I promised," the pallid-faced youngster informed them. "Now Rusty, Dirk Damon and I are going back to Lampasas."

"Give them their guns and let them go," Maudlin authorized, from the doorway. "He's done what he promised and Japhet's going to live."

"By God, *amigo*, you're the cool one!" Rusty breathed, as they went towards their waiting horses. "Or did you reckon Frank was only making wind-talk when he said he'd kill you if Japhet died?"

"I *knew* he meant it," Doc declared.

"Didn't that worry you?" Damon asked.

"Not over much," Doc said quietly, lifting the medical bag in his right hand. "My daddy always kept a loaded and capped Army Colt in here. It's *still* inside—and if Japhet had been dying, *I'd* have known before anybody else."

J. T. EDSON'S FLOATING OUTFIT WESTERN ADVENTURES

J. T. EDSON'S CIVIL WAR SERIES

OTHER BOOKS BY J. T. EDSON

J.T. Edson

DOC LEROY, M.D.

CHARTER BOOKS, NEW YORK

This Charter book contains the complete
text of the original edition.
It has been completely reset in a typeface
designed for easy reading and was printed
from new film.

DOC LEROY, M.D.

A Charter Book/published by arrangement with
Transworld Publishers, Ltd.

PRINTING HISTORY
Corgi edition published 1977
Charter edition/February 1989

ISBN: 1-55773-162-4

Charter Books are published by The Berkley Publishing Group,
200 Madison Avenue, New York, N.Y. 10016.
The name "CHARTER" and the "C" logo are trademarks belonging
to Charter Communications, Inc.

PRINTED IN THE UNITED STATES OF AMERICA

10 9 8 7 6 5 4 3 2 1

*For Brian Whitmore
and the rest of the Doc Leroy syndrome,
who have been bugging me for years to write it.*

Doc Leroy, M.D.

In Explanation

Regular readers of the author's work will no doubt notice certain discrepancies between this volume and the various earlier episodes which featured Marvin Eldridge "Doc" Leroy. When writing Part Two, "Jordan's Try," of THE TOWN TAMERS, for example, I was under the impression that Doc had been attending medical college at the time of his parents' death. However, while attending the 21st Annual Convention of Western Writers of America at Fort Worth, Texas, in 1974 and during a subsequent visit following the 22nd Convention, held in Carson City, Nevada, I was fortunate enough to meet several members of the Hardin, Fog and Blaze clan with whom I had previously only been in written contact. On the latter occasion, as I have never learned to drive,[1] I am indebted to my friends Elley and Chuck Kurtzman of Fort Worth. They not only put me up at their place—and also put up with my horrible "Swiss" jokes—but also supplied me with the "wheels" so vitally necessary when one wishes to travel about in Texas.

Particularly on the second visit, I was chiefly engaged in the task of learning the facts pertaining to the early career of General Jackson Baines "Ole Devil" Hardin[2] and hoping to discover why his Japanese servant, Tommy Okasi,[3] had come

---

1. The author is too modest to suggest that, during his twelve and a half years' service with the Royal Army Veterinary Corps, he was too valuable as a dog trainer to be spared from his duties for long enough to be taught to drive. However, anybody who wishes to think this is at liberty to do so. J.T.E.

2. Details of Jackson Baines "Ole Devil" Hardin's early career are given in the author's *Ole Devil* series. His nickname arose in part from the way he deliberately enhanced the Mephistophelian aspect of his features, but mainly through his reputation among his contemporaries as being a "lil ole devil for a fight". J.T.E.

3. Okasi was not Tommy's real name, but an Americanized corruption of the one he gave when taken aboard the ship captained by General Hardin's father. J.T.E.

to the United States of America never to return to his home-
land. Although I failed to achieve the latter[4], I was fortunate
enough to find out how Doc Leroy continued his education
and why Belle Boyd "The Rebel Spy"[5] required the assistance
of Martha Jane "Calamity Jane"[6] Canary on one of her assign-
ments.[7]

With the help of Alvin Dustine "Cap" Fog[8]—formerly
Captain commanding Company "J" of the Texas Rangers[9]—

4. The author was informed that, because of the circumstances and the
high social standing of the various families involved—all of whom have
descendants holding positions of influence and importance in Japan at the
time of writing—it was inadvisable even at this late date to make the facts
of Tommy Okasi's departure public. J.T.E.

5. Details of Belle Boyd's career are given in: *The Colt and the Sabre;
The Rebel Spy; The Bloody Border; Back to the Bloody Border; The
Hooded Riders; The Bad Bunch; To Arms, To Arms, In Dixie!; The South
Will Rise Again* and *The Quest for Bowie's Blade.* Her sobriquet the
"Rebel Spy" arose out of her activities as an agent for the Confederate
States' Secret Service during the War Between the States and she later
served with distinction as a member of the United States' Secret Service.
The researches of fictionist genealogist Philip José Farmer have estab-
lished that Miss Boyd was the aunt of Lady Jane Greystoke, née Porter,
wife of the 7th Lord Greystoke—who is better known as Tarzan of the
Apes, see various biographies by Edgar Rice Burroughs—and adoptive
mother of James Allenvale "Bunduki" Gunn, some of whose career is
recorded in the author's *Bunduki* series. J.T.E.

6. Miss Martha Jane Canary's career is told in the author's *Calamity Jane*
series. She also makes "guest" appearances in some of the *Floating Outfit*
series. J.T.E.

7. Details of the assignment are given in: *The Whip and the War Lance.*
J.T.E.

8. Permission has now been granted for me to give details of a case in
which Alvin Dustine "Cap" Fog participated in England during 1928.
Told in *Mr. J.G. Reeder, Meet "Cap" Fog!* J.T.E.

9. The Texas Rangers were to all practical purposes abolished on October
17th, 1935, almost one hundred years to the day after their formation.
Their functions were absorbed by the more prosaic Texas Department of
Public Safety and Highway Patrol. In the vernacular of the Civilian Band
radios carried by many private and commercial vehicles, uniformed officers of the latter organization are known as "Smokies" because their
"boy scout" pattern hats resemble the one worn by "Smokey the Bear" on
fire prevention posters. Details of modern Texas law enforcement techniques are given in the author's *Rockabye County* series. J.T.E.

grandson of Captain Dustine Edward Marsden "Dusty" Fog, C.S.A.[10] and no mean combat pistol shot in his own right, I obtained the material which is given in this book. Once again, I apologize for the misconceptions in the earlier titles and assure you that this is the true story of:

DOC LEROY, M.D.

J. T. Edson
Active Member, Western Writers of America
Melton Mowbray, Leics. England

---

10. Details of the career of Captain Dustine Edward Marsden "Dusty" Fog, C.S.A. are given in the author's *Civil War* and *Floating Outfit* series. J.T.E.

PART ONE

Lindrick's Fancy Colts

CHAPTER ONE

I'll Stay Here If *You* Want To

"I'll be eternally damned if I could *ever* take kindly to living in a big city," declared Mrs. Lynn Leroy, nee Baker, formerly —and until very recently—residing in Two Forks, Utah Territory,[1] eyeing her husband in a challenging fashion as they approached the front entrance of the New Orleans' branch of the First National Bank. "Anyways, happen you're a good lil boy, which you shouldn't find no trouble in being now I've got you away from that shiftless, no-account brother-in-law of our'n, and you study real hard at that fancy doctors' school, we shouldn't need to stay on here for all that long."

"Now that's no way to be talking about the honoured, respected and appointed by the popular choice of all the good folks, sheriff of Two Forks County and kind to boot," Marvin Eldridge Leroy protested, his lazy sounding Texan's drawl contrasting with the brisk Mid-Western accent of his bride of three months. "Even if it is all true."

It was doubtful whether the majority of Lynn Leroy's friends and acquaintances would have recognized her if they had been passing at that moment. Her pretty face still retained

1. After having applied and been refused in 1849, '56, '62, '72, '82 and '89—chiefly because the predominantly Mormon population refused, until 1890, to give up the practice of polygamous marriages—Utah was granted Statehood on January the 4th, 1896.

its healthy tan and bore an expression of self confident zest for life. Nor had her five foot seven tall, slender—yet anything but skinny—body lost the grace of movement which told of complete physical fitness.

However, marriage and coming to a major city like New Orleans had brought an end—at least temporarily, she repeatedly told herself—to wearing a man's shirt, trousers, riding boots and gunbelt slanting from her left hip. Instead, a dainty green hat, decorated with a cluster of feathers from the tails of cock Cardinals,[2] was held on her head of shortish black hair by a ribbon tied in a bow under her chin. Her matching jacket-bodice had long, tight sleeves but she eschewed the use of the black lace mittens so many ladies adopted. The overskirt was drawn up at the sides and bunched up at the back, with just a hint of high buttoned shoes peeping from beneath it. As fashion dictated, she had a folded parasol in her right hand. A somewhat larger and more bulky than usual vanity bag's neck was grasped by her left thumb and fingers that augmented the carrying strap around her wrist.

And if it came to a point, many a cowhand with whom Marvin Eldridge Leroy had ridden the range and shared the hazards of trail drives from Texas to the railroad's shipping pens in Kansas would have had to look twice before realizing it was him.

Even in those days of open air living, Marvin Eldridge Leroy's six foot tall, lean frame had been topped by a good looking, somewhat studious face with a tan resistant pallor. It was not altered to any great extent by the neatly trimmed black moustache it now sported. However, gone was his low crowned, broad brimmed J.B. Stetson hat. It was replaced by a brown bowler with a curly brim and high, bowl-shaped crown. His single-breasted brown morning coat, with a narrow collar and short lapels had braided edges to its skirts and

2. Cardinal: *Richmondena Cardinalis*, one of the *Fringillidae* family of seed-eating birds. Apart from the *Pyrrhuloxia* of the South-Western States, the only American bird with a crest and a conical beak. The male's plumage is bright red, but that of the female is a yellowish brown. Frequently caught and sold as a cage pet.

was fastened with four buttons. The vest—waistcoat—was cut straight, the white shirt's collar was high and worn with a dark blue necktie. His trousers were close fitting and the legs narrow at the bottoms. Only his Hessian-leg,[3] high heeled, sharp toed, tan coloured boots remained of his range garb—and no amount of city dwelling could make him discard them—although they no longer carried their Kelly "Pet-Maker" spurs. Probably the most noticeable difference which would have attracted his companions' attention was his lack of armament. His slim, boneless looking hands could draw and shoot a Colt Civilian Model Peacemaker revolver like lightning and with commendable accuracy.

"You wouldn't want to stay on, now would you, Doc?" Lynn inquired, employing her husband's commonly used nickname. Her expression changed and she lost some of the bantering tone from her voice.

"Can't say's I would," the Texan admitted, turning a puzzled gaze on his wife. "What's brought this up, gal?"

"You know's I'd had lunch with Mrs. Dumoulin before I met you?"

"Sure. You wasn't too happy about it this morning."

"Shucks, it wasn't as bad as I expected," Lynn stated. "She's a right nice lady when you get to know her. Anyways, she said her husband was talking about you—"

"It's none of it true," Doc grinned.

"Likely," Lynn answered, but the worried timbre did not leave her speech. "Seeing as how he allowed, being older than most of them, you're a damned sight better—"

"Did Mrs. Dumoulin say *that*?" Doc challenged, squeezing his wife's arm gently.

"Not in so many words," Lynn admitted. "Anyways, as I was saying before you horned in, seeing's you're a whole heap better at doctoring than any of them, he might ask you to stay on as his intern—or whatever it's called—after you qualify."

3. Hessian boots: designed for use by light cavalry such as Hussars, having legs which extend to just below the knee and with a "V" shaped notch at the front.

Although nothing showed on the Texan's face, he was impressed by what he had heard. Being twenty-eight years of age on his last birthday, he was certainly older than any of his fellow students at the Soniat Memorial-Mercy Hospital, where he had recently enrolled to complete his medical studies and, hopefully, qualify as a doctor. In spite of the short time he had been attending the Hospital's medical college, he had a vast amount more practical experience than most of the students. His knowledge on certain matters even exceeded that of some who were awaiting a chance to try for qualification.

All Doc's formative years had been spent in the presence of medical and surgical affairs. His father, Eldridge Jason Leroy, M.D., had been a doctor residing in Lampasas, Texas. As the only qualified practitioner in well over five hundred square miles, Doctor Leroy could not afford the luxury of specializing in one particular field. He needed an equal skill in setting broken bones, supplying cures for various ailments, coping with wounds inflicted by a variety of weapons, handling births and performing surgical operations. In spite of that, being a dedicated and enlightened man, he had done all he could to keep abreast of the latest techniques and developments.

From an early age, the doctor had encouraged his son's interest in the healing arts. Young Doc, as he was soon known locally, had been eager to learn. He was taught anatomy by watching and being allowed to carry out dissections. Then he was instructed in how to diagnose and treat illnesses, detect and repair fractures, and compound medicinal potions. He had gathered much knowledge and retained it with a degree of capability that had augured well for the future.

At the same time, growing up in an area devoted exclusively to the cattle business, Doc had found time—his father being a firm believer that "all work and no play made Jack a dull boy"—to acquire many of the cowhands' skills. One in particular, the ability he gained as a horseman, would be of great use to him in his chosen field of endeavour. It provided the quickest way to travel the great distances involved when making house calls on the open ranges where he would find the majority of his patients. So his father had been pleased to see him become an accomplished rider.

When circumstances had forced Doc to become a cow-hand, almost the only means of making an honest living in Texas during the impoverished years following the War Between the States, he had contrived to keep up his studies.

And more!

Working as a member of Stone Hart's crew of contract trail herders, on ranches and, later, serving with the Arizona Rangers,[4] Doc had frequently been required to turn his knowledge to practical use. His skill had firmly saddled him with the sobriquet by which even his wife invariably referred to him. There were men, women and children who would have been dead, or unborn, without his assistance.

Sometimes, with the passing of the years, Doc had become almost resigned to the thought that he would never achieve his ambition to follow in his father's footsteps. However, after the events at the town of Two Forks had culminated in his marriage to Lynn,[5] the opportunity was at last presented to him and in a way which he would have found very difficult to refuse.

As a wedding present from a former employer, Doc had received an offer of enrollment at the Medical College of the Soniat Memorial-Mercy Hospital in New Orleans. On hearing this, Ella Baker—his charming, beautiful, but exceptionally forceful-natured mother-in-law—had exerted her persuasive powers, not that they had been entirely necessary, towards convincing him that only good could come from accepting the offer. In addition, without causing embarrassment or resentment, she had helped to remove any financial barriers which might have accrued, and had assuaged Lynn's understandable concern over the prospect of being compelled to live for an indefinite period in a large city.

On his arrival, Doc had been informed by the Dean of the Medical College that he could commence his education at the point to which his knowledge entitled him. This meant that because of his learning and experience, he was already almost

---

4. Details of Doc Leroy's service with the Arizona Rangers is given in: *Sagebrush Sleuth*, *Arizona Ranger* and *Waco Rides In*.
5. Told in: *The Drifter*.

capable of sitting for the final qualifying examinations. Doc had a strong suspicion that General Jackson Baines "Ole Devil" Hardin,[6] notwithstanding the fact that he was confined to a wheelchair since being crippled in a riding accident,[7] had applied his considerable influence upon the normally stuffy and conservative Doctor Alphonse Jules Dumoulin and had helped bring about such a concession.

Since coming to New Orleans, Doc had been concerned over the life he was causing Lynn to lead. Her formative years had been spent on a small ranch in Wyoming. Following the separation of her parents, when she had remained in her father's custody, her upbringing had been closer to that of a boy than a girl. Many of her friends at that period had been prominent members of the outlaw fraternity, and from them she had received an unconventional—yet under the circumstances, eminently practical education. Even after her father's death when she had gone to live with her mother, she had known only the environment of a small Western town. However, Ella had contrived to instil in her the acceptable social graces. Although she had objected at the time, she was finding them to be of great benefit at present.

Because of Doc's studies, Lynn was compelled to spend much of the day without his company. However, once again, one of their friends had come to their aid. Envisaging the situation, Captain Dustine Edward Marsden "Dusty" Fog[8] had given them a letter of introduction to the New Orleans Police Department's recently appointed Captain of Detectives. Phillipe St. Andre, who was known as "Sherry" to his friends,[9] and his wife had made the young couple welcome. Nor had their kindness merely been due to St. Andre owing his promotion, at least partly, to information received from the Rio Hondo gun wizard.[10]

6. How this influence was earned is told in the *Ole Devil Hardin* and *Civil War* series. See Footnote 2 of the "In Explanation" section on Page vii.
7. Told in "The Paint" episode of: *The Fastest Gun In Texas*.
8. See Footnote 10 of the "In Explanation" section on Page ix.
9. How Captain Phillipe St. Andre had acquired his nickname, before his promotion, is told in: *The Bullwhip Breed*.
10. How this came about is told in: *The Man From Texas*.

Taking Lynn under her wing and to her heart, Alice St. Andre had kept her from growing lonely or bored. In addition to showing her the sights and introducing her to friends, Alice had also steered her clear of the social pitfalls which might otherwise have happened to ruin her stay. By way of repayment, using lessons acquired from professional gamblers with whom she was acquainted, Lynn had exposed a couple of female card sharps who had been taking large sums of money from wealthy ladies—and some who could ill afford the losses—by cheating at whist.

"A man could do a whole heap worse than that, gal," Doc remarked and felt his wife's bicep tense under his hand. "Doctor Dumoulin's well thought of in medical circles all through the country."

"I'm not gainsaying it," Lynn admitted quietly.

"Being his intern wouldn't pay as much as I could likely make back home in Two Forks," Doc went on. "Nor would any other post in the hospital for a fair spell to come. Against that, if anything new is learned, it'll be heard about sooner at the hospital."

"I'll stay here if *you* want to," Lynn stated and tried to sound more enthusiastic as she went on, "Shucks, I might even get to like it."

Before the conversation could be taken any further, the couple reached the open double doors of the bank. Walking through, they found themselves to be the only customers. Behind the grills, the tellers were totalling up their cash. The bank guard, a burly man in a blue uniform who carried a Colt Cavalry Peacemaker in a closed topped holster from which, Doc decided, he would be able to draw it in something less than a minute—but not much—if the need to do so rapidly should arise, looked pointedly at the clock on the wall.

"You reckon he's trying to tell us it's just about time for them to close for the day?" Lynn inquired, temporarily putting aside the matter that was uppermost in her mind, as her husband removed his hand from her arm.

"Could be," Doc admitted and reached into his jacket. Then he gave an annoyed grunt. "Blast it! I've not made out a withdrawal draft. How much will you want, honey?"

"Nothing," Lynn replied, following her husband to a writing table against the left side wall. "I'm putting some in, not taking it out."

"Huh?" Doc ejaculated.

"Why sure, that's why I sent word for you to meet me and come here," Lynn grinned. "Seems like all those ladies were sort of grateful to me for catching out those two female card sharps. Especially as Sherry found they'd still got most all of the money and the notes-of-hand they'd taken and would've been turning in for payment."

"Go on, blast you!" Doc commanded, when his wife stopped and looked at him provocatively. "What *happened*?"

"I thought you'd *never* ask. Well, it seems like they got to thinking, you being a medical student and all, that we likely aren't busting at the seams with money right now. So they'd collected five hundred simoleons as a reward."

"And you *took* it?" Doc asked, swinging his gaze around.

"You can bet your Texas hide I did!" Lynn answered, stiffening a little and meeting his glare without flinching. "Which, seeing's how Sherry got back at least ten times that much cash, not counting the notes that'd been signed, I reckon I was entitled to it."

"Whooee!" Doc breathed. Although he had heard about the incident, he had no idea that such a large sum of money was involved. Nor was he too proud to appreciate that their bank balance could stand such a replenishment. "Do you mean you're toting all that cash on you right now?"

"Why sure," Lynn confirmed and lifted her vanity bag. "You don't figure I'd be toting *this* one if all I had on me was my girlie face-fixings, do you?"

"Nope, I don't reckon you would," Doc conceded, without admitting that he had not noticed which of her vanity bags she was carrying. Knowing what must be in it, apart from the money, he continued, "Shucks, you don't figure you'd be likely to need *that*. Not in a fancy big city like New Orleans."

"I don't expect I will," Lynn answered, just a touch defiantly. "But one thing I learned real early. Happen I should need it, there won't be time to go back to the apartment and fetch it."

Under different conditions, Doc would have expressed his complete concurrence with his wife's statment. However, as they were talking, he noticed five men coming in. From their appearance and the fact that they had arrived on horseback, leaving the animals fastened to the hitching posts provided for use by the bank's customers, he judged them to be country dwellers paying a visit to the city. All were clad in cheap store bought suits and, despite the clement early summer weather, were wearing unfastened cloak-coats into the capacious pockets of which each had at least one hand thrust. The broad brimmed hats they wore were drawn down so that, either by accident or design, their faces were partially concealed.

The fourth and fifth men to enter stepped to either side of the doors and halted with their backs against the wall. While the one at the right looked down, the other gazed about him. Tall, lean and, Doc observed, wearing a pair of cowhand boots, he was in his early twenties and had a weak face set in what he probably regarded as a tough expression.

After advancing a couple of strides beyond the threshold, the tallest of the new arrivals glanced to his left and nodded. As if he had received a signal, the man nearest to Doc and Lynn started walking in their direction. Stepping out more briskly, the last of the quintet converged on the bank guard as he approached the couple with the intention of hinting that it was time for the establishment to close.

There was something significant about the newcomers' actions, Doc realized. Yet he could hardly believe that what it reminded him of was going to happen.

In a Western town, such behaviour would have suggested that the quintet intended to rob the bank.

Of course, the same could not apply in an Eastern city the size of New Orleans.

Or could it?

CHAPTER TWO

All They Aim to Do Is Rob Us

Even as Doc Leroy was forming his summations regarding the five new arrivals, he received an answer to them which removed any possibility of doubt. Each produced a weapon—in the case of the young hard-case at the left side of the main entrance, two comparatively small, yet fine looking revolvers which might be the type known as the Colt Pocket Pistol of Navy Calibre,[1] but rechambered to fire .36 metallic cartridges —from the pockets of the cloak-coats.

"All right, everybody!" growled the tallest of the quintet, gesturing with the especially effective firearm that he had extracted. It was a ten gauge shotgun with the barrels cut down to about twelve inches and the butt foreshortened by removing it behind the wrist. His tones were a hard Texas drawl and, Doc noticed, like the young man, he had on range boots. "Just stand still, keep quiet and nobody'll get hurt."

"Wha—?" croaked the bank guard, head swivelling around and right hand moving spasmodically towards the closed flap of the unsuitable holster.

"Don't try it!" warned the man who had obviously been assigned to prevent such an intervention. He made a menacing

1. Sometimes erroneously called the Colt Model of 1853 revolver, made with four and a half, five and a half, or six and a half inch barrels.

gesture with his Colt Cavalry Model Peacemaker.

Much to Doc's relief, the guard refrained from attempting the ill-advised attempt to reach his weapon. Equally fortunately, in the Texan's experienced opinion, although the tellers were staring in open mouthed amazement, none of them was offering to do anything other than obey the order they had been given. He hoped they would continue to do so. Employees in a similar establishment west of the Mississippi River would have sufficient knowledge of the danger to behave sensibly. The men behind the counter at the New Orleans' branch of the First National Bank were unlikely to possess such an acquaintance with this kind of situation and might not appreciate just how lethally dangerous these men could be.

With those thoughts racing through his head, Doc forced himself to remember that he was no longer wearing a gun. Since putting it aside on his arrival in New Orleans, he had gradually become accustomed to the omission from carrying out something that had been as much a part of his life as donning his other garments each morning. Just as he had never been actively conscious of the ivory handled Colt Civilian Model Peacemaker—or even its heavier[2] Colt 1860 Army revolver predecessor—hanging at his right thigh in those days, he had now almost stopped realizing it was no longer on his person.

Keeping that vitally important fact in mind, Doc studied the weapon in the hand of the man who had approached and who was covering himself and his wife. He noticed, and did not doubt that Lynn had also, that the hammer of the Merwin & Hulbert Army Pocket revolver was in the down position. That, as he realized—and hoped Lynn did too—was not as advantageous as it might appear to be. Unlike the makers'

2. The Colt Civilian Model Peacemaker—which had a four and three-quarter inch barrel as opposed to five and a half for the "Artillery" and seven and a half for the "Cavalry" Models—weighed two pounds four ounces, the 1860 Army two pounds eleven ounces.

Model 1876 "Army"[3] revolver from which it had been derived, the short barrelled—three and five-sixteenths of an inch, as opposed to seven inches—"Pocket" variety had a double action mechanism which did not require cocking manually before it would operate.

"Now don't *anybody* do anything reckless," Doc advised, in a loud voice. He was directing the words mainly at his wife, who had already moved her right hand so that it was in the mouth of the vanity bag without receiving any response from the man with the Merwin & Hulbert revolver. "If all they aim to do is rob us, I'd say it makes right good sense to let them."

"Well now," sneered the young two gun toter. "Comes us going, could be we'll take us a right pretty lil gal along's—"

"Shut your damned fool mouth, Blaby!" the tallest of the quintet commanded savagely, but without looking back or allowing his shotgun to waver. In a quieter, yet no less threatening tone, he went on, "That gent's making right good sense, fellers. Why get shot to hell and gone when all that'll be lost is *somebody else's* money."

To Doc's relief the tellers and bank guard took the advice. All too well he realized the danger they were all facing. Apart from the spokesman, none of the five struck him as being the kind of criminals who had made a regular habit of indulging in such an enterprise. With the exception of the young man by the door, they had the appearance of city dwellers. Raising their heads had shown pallid faces in comparison with the tanned visages of the pair wearing range boots. Capable as they might be in a brawl involving bare hands, feet and other rudimentary weapons, their knowledge of firearms was liable to be limited.

If shooting started, such men would be inclined to go hog-

---

3. Used in this context, the term "Army" refers to the calibre: .44 of an inch. Despite the military's derisive assertion that it was easier to kill a sailor than a soldier, the "Navy's" .36 calibre was selected so that the revolvers' weight—which would have to be carried on the seaman's belt, rather than by a man who would generally be riding a horse; hand guns having been originally and primarily developed for use by members of the cavalry—could be held at an acceptable level.

wild and throw lead indiscriminately. However, any deficiencies in ability would be offset—at least by the pair covering Lynn, Doc and the guard—through them being so close that they would be unlikely to miss.

Nor would the loud-mouthed young Westerner hesitate before starting to shoot. In fact, unless Doc was misjudging his character, he was all too eager to do so. Innocent and defenceless people were likely to die if that happened. Neither the tellers nor—the Texan suspected—the guard possessed enough experience in this situation to take the requisite evasive action.

Relatively satisfied on one point, Doc turned a quick look at his wife. Her right hand was already inside the neck of the vanity bag and, although the man in front of them had not noticed anything was amiss, had closed around the finely checked rosewood handle of the two and a half inch barreled .41 Colt Thunderer revolver which had been a birthday present—accompanied by a note that it should help to ensure she had no difficulty in making himself behave—from their brother-in-law and his former Ranger partner, Waco.[4] He had, in turn, made a similar gift, for the same reason, to Lynn's twin sister, Waco's wife, Beth.

Doc knew that Lynn was extremely competent in the use of firearms and had already learned how to utilize the compact, powerful Thunderer to its best advantage. What was more, she would—if necessary—turn its lethal potential against another human being; a very different proposition from shooting holes in the bull's-eye of a lifeless target.

Catching her husband's glance, Lynn gave a quick and confirmatory nod. It told him all he needed to know. She was already holding the Thunderer and, despite it having a double action mechanism, was drawing back the hammer with her thumb. However, she had paralleled his deductions and summation of the situation. So she had no intention of using the weapon, for all that it was still unsuspected by the man who was closest to them, unless something happened to compel her to change her mind. Much as she hated the thought of losing the five hundred dollars in the bag, she was willing to do so rather than jeopardize the lives of the other occupants of the bank.

"Get those doors closed, Blaby, Tick!" the tallest of the gang called over his shoulder. "And you gents back there start piling the money on the counter. That's all we want, nothing belonging to you, or you two young folks."

Before the order could be obeyed, footsteps sounded on the sidewalk.

A well dressed couple about Doc's and Lynn's age entered the building. Just across the threshold, they came to a halt. Clearly they could tell that something was wrong, but were unable to decide exactly what it might be.

Instantly, Doc knew that there was going to be trouble!

Grinning wolfishly, Blaby hooked his gun-filled left hand under the woman's arm and jerked her further into the room. A startled and frightened squeal burst from her as she felt what was happening.

"What the—?" began the newly arrived man, turning his head and, without wasting as much as a second to consider the danger, he lunged towards the woman's assailant. "Let go o—!"

Still exhibiting his leer of triumph, Blaby jerked free his hand. However, it was not with the intention of complying with the man's demand. Instead, he turned up his second weapon and squeezed the trigger. Obviously the revolver had been cocked, for it spat viciously. Either luck or skill guided the conical .36 bullet in a most advantageous manner.

Hit anywhere except a couple of vital points in the body, particularly as he was large and powerful and angry over his wife's mistreatment, the man might have kept his feet for long enough to reach and grapple with the young outlaw. As it was, although the bullet did no more than strike his head a glancing blow, he was sent in a spinning stagger sideways. Like the woman, who had been shoved hard enough to make her lose her footing, he went sprawling to the floor.

Hearing the commotion, all the three outlaws furthest into

the room looked behind them to find out what had caused it. By the door, Tick—who, along with Blaby, was the youngest of the gang and had been left there to help with the most simple task—stared as if he could hardly believe the evidence of his eyes.

Taking in the sight, Doc knew the thing he had feared was happening!

The young Texan was equally aware of what must be done!

Nor was there even a split second to spare before taking action!

Without sparing Lynn so much as a glance, but hoping she would know what to do, Doc went into action. Despite an urgent need to arm himself, he ignored the nearest man. He had never handled a Merwin & Hulbert revolver and, faced with such a desperate emergency, wanted a weapon much closer to the one he knew best. To achieve his aim, he lunged for the outlaw who was covering the bank guard.

As he was commencing his move, Doc realized that the success of his strategy depended on his faith in his wife's judgment. If she failed to come up to his expectations, he would soon know about it.

And, in all probability, be killed!

Thinking as Doc had hoped she would, Lynn guessed how he would react and realized he was counting on her to support him. The instant he moved, she started to snatch the concealed Thunderer from the vanity bag. She was already pointing it in the general direction of the man in front of them. As he was beginning to turn his weapon after Doc, his forefinger applying the pressure needed to cock the action, she did not want to take the Colt out of alignment even for an instant if it could be avoided.

The bag and the revolver appeared to have become entangled!

Stabbing forward his left hand, Doc grabbed the frame and cylinder of the man's Cavalry Model Peacemaker. Working in perfect conjunction, his clenched right fist drove out. Hard knuckles rammed into the centre of the outlaw's face. Half blinded by tears and pain, with blood starting to flow from his nostrils, he went backwards a couple of steps. More important, as far as his assailant was concerned, he relaxed his hold on his weapon.

Although Doc twisted the Colt from its owner's grasp, he still had to manipulate it into a firing position.

Giving a savage tug, Lynn liberated the Thunderer. Taking not the slightest notice of the money which was spewing from it, her left hand flung the vanity bag aside. She now had the means to play her part.

All her life, Lynn had known desperate and dangerous men. She had learned early not to flinch from any action that might be necessary to safeguard herself or those she loved. So, although the man was looking away from her, she had no compunction over what she intended to do. At that moment, all traces of her civilized behaviour had fled. She was a pure, primeval female seeking to protect her mate.

Continuing to advance for three strides, Doc flashed down his right hand to wrap around the Colt's butt. As he was doing so, he began to swivel in the direction of the man he considered to be most dangerous.

Squeezing the trigger, Lynn had the advantage of the hammer already being at full cock. Relieved of the sear's restraint, it lashed forward. The Thunderer's short barrel caused it to live up to its name when fired. For all that, the man could count himself fortunate to take the bullet in his shoulder. She had not aimed deliberately to achieve such a comparatively mild injury. Letting out a shriek of pain, he spun away from her and, dropping his weapon, collapsed with both hands clutching at the wound.

With the crash of the Thunderer, and the screech from its victim ringing in his ears, informing him that Lynn had justified his confidence, Doc came to a halt adopting what was already known as a gun fighter's crouch. With his feet spread apart and legs slightly bent, he inclined his body forward at the waist and thrust out his newly acquired weapon. Its extra six ounces of weight and two and three-quarters inches longer barrel gave it a different balance to the Colt Civilian Model Peacemaker which had served him so well in the past. However, it possessed the same kind of excellently shaped butt, the most natural pointing grip ever fitted to a hand gun.

One glance was all Doc needed to warn him that there was no time for fancy shooting, or even to take a careful aim. Speed was of the most vital urgency. Looking around, the tallest and most dangerous of the quintet had discovered where their most pressing threat was situated. Although the muzzles of the shotgun were pointing in the opposite direction, he was swinging them to correct their alignment.

Nor, although Doc did not know it, was that the only menace to him!

The man who had been deprived of his revolver had come to a halt and was far from incapacitated in spite of a throbbing and bleeding nose. His vision had cleared to give him a view of his assailant. Realizing that the Texan's attention was directed elsewhere, he spat out a curse and lunged forward with hands lifting to grab.

Seeing what his actions had brought about, Blaby was more pleased than perturbed as he sought to play his part in rectifying the situation. Twisting his lips into a sadistic sneer, he raised his right hand Colt so that he could take sight along its octagonal four and a half inch barrel.

Blaby was experiencing a sense of savage exultation over the thought that, by shooting down the "dude" who was interfering with their plan, he would have achieved a long cherished ambition not once but twice. To have put lead into two men was, in his estimation, a feat worthy of such great owlhoots as the James or Younger brothers. It would prove once and for all—even his acquisition of the two revolvers had failed to do so—to Big Hadle that he too was a real bad *hombre*. The next time they pulled a hold up together, he would not be assigned to the menial task of waiting by and closing the doors.

Succour was at hand for Doc, from two sources.

No gun fighter, his revolver having been supplied more as a potential threat than with any idea that he might need to use it, the bank guard was still a brave man with a sense of duty. Making no attempt to draw the weapon, he flung himself at the outlaw Doc had disarmed. Tackling him around the waist with all the power of a burly and hard body, the guard knocked and went to the floor with him.

Although Lynn had removed the closest source of danger, she did not consider that the affair was over. In fact, she was aware that there might still be need for her to give Doc further support. So her gaze had been sweeping around the room. With a far greater knowledge than the guard of such corpse-and-cartridge occasions, she decided that she must leave the man with the shotgun to her husband. Discovering what Blaby was attempting had told her that. She had formed an accurate estimation of his character and had guessed he would be the one to require her attention.

In fact, his actions were already demanding it!

And with the minimum of delay!

Assessing his predicament, Doc knew the only way in which he could deal with it. No single action revolver could attain the speed of fire possible with a double action mechanism,[5] but there was a means by which one could be emptied at a much faster rate than by conventional methods.

Pressing his right elbow tightly against his side for increased firmness and control, Doc aligned the barrel in the general direction of the man with the shotgun. Flashing across, the heel of his left hand took a circular motion which made contact and drew the hammer rearwards. Without the need for conscious guidance, his right forefinger was already depressing the trigger. On being released, the hammer returned and set off the cartridge in the cylinder's uppermost chamber.

"Fanning," as the method being employed by Doc was called, did not allow for anywhere near the kind of accuracy that could be attained by more formal shooting. So he was not surprised when his first shot missed. Even while he was con-

5. The fastest recorded rate of fire for a manually operated double action mechanism occurred on January 23rd, 1934, at Lewiston, Montana. Using a Smith & Wesson revolver, Ed. McGivern fired *five* shots into a playing card at eighteen feet in *two-fifths* of a second. See *Fast and Fancy Revolver Shooting* by Ed. McGivern.

trolling the Colt's recoil kick as well as he could manage, he altered the angle at which the barrel was pointing slightly.

Flame erupted from the Colt's muzzle for a second time as Doc's left hand continued its motions, then a third, a fourth and a fifth. Between each detonation, brief though the period might be, he had turned the weapon so that the lead was flying in a fan-like pattern. Fortunately, there was nobody behind the man at whom he was firing and he did not need to worry about endangering innocent bystanders.

Refusing to be distracted by the rolling beat of her husband's borrowed weapon, Lynn cupped her left palm under the gun-filled right hand. Elevating the Thunderer to eye-level, while her right thumb drew back its hammer, she aimed at the young outlaw at the door. He fired before she could press the trigger.

Aware that his shotgun was still not far enough around to be used, Hadle was conscious of the two bullets that had winged their way by him. They had been thrown by the smoke-wrapped, lean and city-dressed *hombre* who nevertheless handled the Colt like a top hand gun fighter trained in matters *pistolero* somewhere west of the Big Muddy.[6]

The second shot had been much closer than its predecessor and the outlaw knew more were coming. Then he felt himself struck by the third. Even as he was rocked by the impact, he was hit twice more in *very* rapid succession.[7] Pitched backwards, he tightened his forefinger on the shotgun's trigger. Although it discharged, he was already falling and the barrels were tilting upwards. So the nine buckshot balls flew harmlessly into the ceiling. The weapon tumbled from his hands as he measured his length on the floor.

Blaby had just realized that his attempt to kill the "dude"

6. Big Muddy: colloquial name for the Mississippi River, by tradition the dividing line between the "civilized" East and the "frontier" West.
7. Ed. McGivern, q.v., fired four five-shot fanning volleys in respectively one and two-fifths, one and three-tenths, one and a quarter and one and a fifth seconds; placing each set of bullets in an area slightly larger than his hand. While Doc Leroy was almost as fast, he was shooting under much more demanding conditions and at a somewhat longer range.

had missed when Lynn cut loose at him. Once again, she scored a less devastating hit than would have been attained if she could have taken a more careful aim. However, it served her purpose. Instead of taking him in the head, the Thunderer's bullet did no more than tear off his hat.

It also gave the young outlaw one hell of a shock!

For all his aura of toughness, Blaby had never been under fire. Realizing how narrow an escape he had had, he lost his nerve. Dropping the revolvers with a howl of fright, he spun around and dived through the door.

Less hardened as a criminal than any of his companions, Tick had been growing aware that their enterprise was going horrifyingly wrong. So he needed no more than Blaby's example to decide upon what he should do. Throwing away the revolver he had been loaned for the robbery, he followed his fleeing companion.

Much to their increased terror, the two young men discovered that the sound of the shooting was attracting attention. Already people, including two big and brawny police officers, were running from both directions. Darting to the waiting horses, the pair saw that these might not offer them the kind of immediate means of escape they so desperately required. When securing the animals, they had tied the reins in knots. Disturbed by the commotion, the horses had tried to escape. In doing so, they had tightened their bonds.

"Come on!" Blaby shrieked, having unpleasant memories of how the enraged citizens of a Western town he had been in treated outlaws caught robbing its bank. "Run for it!"

Tick needed no urging. Springing away from the horses, he fled across the street. With Blaby hot on his heels, he dashed down an alley. He knew that their only hope of salvation was to reach the dock area. Having grown up there, he could find a safe hiding place until he could arrange to leave New Orleans.

Swivelling around as the outlaw fell, Doc was ready to defend himself against whoever had shot at him. Before he could do so, Lynn's intervention had caused the two men at the door's departure. A glance told him that the guard, who was straddling the outlaw's chest and cracking his head with some force against the unyielding floor, needed no help. So he darted across the room.

Approaching the door, Doc glanced at the revolers dropped by the fleeing Blaby.

The closer sight of them brought the Texan to a halt!

CHAPTER THREE

What'd You See in There?

Oblivious of the fact that the two outlaws were certain to be continuing their flight, Doc Leroy stood and stared downwards.

The two revolvers discarded by the young outlaw, Blaby, were—as Doc had guessed—exceptionally fine examples of the type advertised by their manufacturer as the Colt Pocket Pistol of Navy Calibre; which had been rechambered—possibly by the makers' designer, Charles B. Richards—to take a metallic cartridge instead of the original percussion cap, powder and ball. The frames and barrels were of the Best Citizens Finish blueing and engraved with elegant scroll work. What was more, the cylinder which had replaced the original was also unfluted and had a similar hold-on scene etched around it. Each set of ivory stocks bore the letters H.P.L. intertwined on what would be the outside when held in the correct hand suggesting that they were a matched pair.

Although that particular product of the Colt Patent Arms Manufacturing Company would not even come close to matching the number of the various types and calibres of the 1873 Model P "Peacemaker" which had been sold,[1] they were

1. Including the "Target" and "Bisley" varieties, over 600,000 Colt Model P's were made before production, which had commenced in 1873, was discontinued in 1941; mainly because the Company wished to devote all its facilities to the manufacture of more modern firearms for use by the Allies in World War II. Popular demand caused production to be resumed in 1955, with no major changes in design or finish.

far from a rarity. However, the three letters on the butt were enough to make Doc sure that he would identify their owner previous to them having come into Blaby's possession. He realized that it was possible somebody with identical initials could also have purchased a pair of the Pocket Pistols equipped with ivory stocks, but the odds were astronomically against it.

The two revolvers might have been fitted with their original cap and ball cylinders when Doc had last come into contact with them, but he felt sure that he knew to whom they had belonged. Nor had they changed hands too long ago. He doubted whether, even if a succession of owners had had them, the most recent—the young outlaw who had dropped them as he fled—was the kind of person to have retained them in their present excellent condition for any extensive period.

Having started to follow her husband, kicking the Merwin & Hulbert Army Pocket revolver belonging to the man she had wounded across the room and beyond his reach in passing, Lynn Leroy stared in amazement. Whilst she knew much about the circumstances which had brought an end to his earlier hopes of attending a medical college and completing his education, she would never have imagined what was causing him to behave the way he was.

Despite there being such an element of coincidence that no writer of fiction would dare to use in one of his plots, Doc had known the original owner of the matched brace of Colts.

Nor was it surprising that the Texan had recognized them!

A man did not easily forget the person who had been responsible for the death of his parents!

Doc could not even start to visualize the turn of fate which had, after so many years, brought him into contact with a man who was carrying Hayden Paul Lindrick's two Colts. He was aware of the superstitious regard in which their original owner had held them. It was unlikely that anybody else would have gone to the trouble and not inconsiderable expense to have them converted so they would fire the more modern type of ammunition. No ordinary set of circumstances would have persuaded Den Lindrick to part with them.

Reminding himself that the man who could solve the mystery was close by, but was trying to get away, Doc prepared to give chase. However, his training as a peace officer and exceptionally proficient gun fighter refused to let him behave in a reckless and unthinking manner. Both of the fleeing outlaws had dropped their revolvers, but either might still be armed with a hitherto undisclosed weapon of some kind.

Counting instinctively as he had been fanning off the shots, Doc knew that the Colt he was holding had at the most one more bullet and might even be empty. So he let it slip from his grasp. Snatching up what should have been the left side Pocket Pistol, as the feel of the initials on the stock against the fingers of his right hand informed him, he lunged through the door. One glance at the five still rearing and frightened horses told him all he needed to know. Gazing around, he was just in time to see Blaby and Tick running into the alley across the street.

On the point of going after Doc out of the bank, Lynn noticed that the other woman was kneeling and staring at the man who had accompanied her. There was blood flowing from the side of his skull, but not enough for him to have received a direct hit *in* the head. Nor would his chest still be rising and falling as he breathed if he had, although the slight twitching of his limbs could still be happening so soon after death.

No matter how lucky the man had been, Lynn knew that he needed medical attention as quickly as possible.

Bearing that thought in mind, Lynn darted out of the building. She found that Doc was crossing the sidewalk in pursuit of the rapidly departing outlaws. A quick glance to her left and right supplied the information that several men, including two members of the New Orleans Police Department were doing the same thing.

"Doc!" Lynn yelled, skidding to a halt. "Leave the johnlaws to chase them. There's a bad hurt man in here needing you."

The sound of his wife's voice reached Doc as he was leaping from the sidewalk and trying to decide whether to try to liberate one of the horses as a means of speeding his pursuit. What the words implied struck him immediately. Much as he wanted to catch the man who might be able to solve the mystery that was plaguing him, he still had the instincts of a doctor.

There was another reason why Doc should not keep up the chase, apart from such humanistic considerations. It was based upon his experiences as a peace officer. While he had spent many of his leisure hours in the company of Captain Phillipe St. Andre and had given a demonstration of gun fighting techniques for members of the New Orleans Police Department, not every officer had been able to attend. If the pair who were approaching had been absent during the display, they were unlikely to recognize him. Seeing him running from the bank, armed in such a fashion, they could draw a dangerously erroneous conclusion. Neither held a revolver, but he had seen how effective some of their colleagues could send a night-stick spinning through the air to bring down a fleeing fugitive. Like Blaby, he appreciated the danger from a mob of aroused citizens. If he should be felled in what they regarded as an attempt to flee from the crime he had been committing, they might not give him an opportunity to explain.

Finally, the two policemen had in all probability been walking their beats in this area for long enough to have a vastly greater knowledge of its geography than Doc possessed. In which case, they stood a far better chance of hunting the two outlaws through the back streets. Their chances would be increased if they did not have to delay either to deal with him, or to listen to an explanation of his presence.

"Go after them, gents!" Doc called, coming to a halt and allowing the Colt to dangle muzzle downwards. He addressed the words to the policemen, who were already changing their direction so as to converge with him. "I'll take care of things inside."

With relief, the Texan saw the nearer officer wave confirmation with a night-stick loaded hand. Then, as the pair resumed their original route towards the alley, there was the sound of rapidly approaching hooves and wheels.

Turning his head, Doc let out a low grunt of satisfaction, surprise and relief intermingled. Coming along the street at a fast pace were four riders. Behind them, the driver of a New Orleans Police Department's "paddy wagon"[2] was urging his four-horse team to gallop as swiftly as possible. Even without that much of a clue, the Texan would have known that reinforcements of the best possible kind were on hand. The horsemen were "Sherry" St. Andre and members of his Bureau of Detectives.

"Good for Sherry!" Lynn enthused, as her husband walked towards her. "Only how did he get here so handy and useful?"

"Likely we'll soon enough get told," the Texan replied.

"What's wrong, honey?" Lynn asked worriedly, reading the perturbation behind Doc's almost expressionless features and in the timbre of his voice. Remembering how he had come to such an abrupt halt inside the building, she went on, "What'd you see in there?"

"I'll tell you later," the Texan answered. "Go back in there and pick up your bag, it's got all your ill-gotten gains in it. I'll wait for Sher—"

"*You'll* come in and take a look at that wounded man!" Lynn declared in the tone which her husband had learned to know meant she would accept no refusal. "Sherry'll know where to find you and there's enough of them so you won't be needed in the posse."

"That's just what I was thinking," Doc drawled and reversed the Colts, holding them forward. "Here, take these and keep them for me, honey. These folks likely haven't seen a doctor toting a brace of hog-legs."

"They're more like 'shoat-legs'," Lynn sniffed, extending her left forefinger and hooking it through the two trigger-guards. A "shoat" was a small, or baby pig. "Real fancy lil things, though, aren't they?"

"*Real* fancy," Doc conceded and again something in his demeanour drew his wife's eyes to his face. As she glanced down at the Colts, then lifted her gaze once more, he went on, "I'll tell you in a while, honey."

---

2. Paddy wagon: a large patrol wagon designed to transport a number of officers or prisoners. The name is said to have originated in New York because the majority of passengers in both categories were Irish.

"Huh huh!" Lynn grunted, knowing that the matter was *very* important to her husband, but not of absolute urgency.

Returning to the inside of the bank, the young couple found that the manager and the tellers had come from behind the counter. The former, showing alarm and concern, was with the other woman at the side of the wounded man. Some of the latter were gathered around the bank guard and the two living outlaws, but two were picking up Lynn's money. None of them were anywhere near the corpse of the man Doc had killed.

"I—er—That is I—!" the manager began, clearly feeling that he should make some comment and yet unable to put his thoughts into words. He was a small, plump, pompous-featured middle-aged man and his face showed he had been badly shaken by the recent events. "The ba—I—!"

"Best let me take a look at the wound, ma'am," Doc suggested, ignoring the bank official and kneeling at the woman's side. "I'm not a qualified doctor yet, but I'm a senior student over to the Soniat Memorial-Mercy Hospital."

Although the Texan did not mention the fact, he had had more practical experience in the treatment of gun shot wounds than the majority of the qualified doctors at the Hospital. Nor did he wait for permission before reaching out and cupping his left hand under the injured man's head and raising it from the woman's knee. Staring at him through her tear-reddened and frightened eyes, she raised no objections. In fact, she seemed grateful for the chance of assistance and was disinclined to dispute his right to render it. Under the circumstances, as he realized, she would have been willing to let any competent looking person help her. However, she did not offer to move away from her husband.

"Here!" Lynn said to the bank's manager, seeing what was happening and offering him the three weapons. "Hold on to these for me."

"Wha—?" the official yelped, drawing his hands away and with an expression of horror coming to his face. "You—?"

"They won't bite you, blast it, nor go off even, unless you cock the hammers and squeeze the triggers—Or *drop* them!" Lynn promised, the last three words being uttered as she thrust the revolvers into the man's reluctant grasp. They produced the desired effect, for he clutched the weapons and allowed her to devote her attention to something of more importance at that moment. Bending and giving a nod to her husband, she hooked her hands under the other woman's armpits. Lifting gently, she went on, "Up you come now, honey. There's nothing you can do down there except get in Doc's way. And don't you worry none. He's smarter than he looks—Which I reckon you'll agree he'd *have* to be."

Gasping as she felt herself being lifted with a strength that —without being harsh or forceful—she could not resist, particularly in her present condition, the woman looked at the speaker. She saw a pretty face with such an air of complete assurance that she felt herself growing calmer. Glancing down, she found that the slim young man had taken on the support of her husband.

Resting the man's back against his bent left knee, Doc studied the wound to satisfy himself that his first impression had been correct. It was a bloody furrow, but neither too wide nor deep. For all that, he knew it could be more serious than merely a nasty looking graze. There was a possibility that the skull had been fractured by the impact. Or other complications might have resulted from what, despite having glanced off, must have been a hard blow.

While making his closer examination, Doc followed his father's advice. "Eyes first, hands as little as possible and questions, if they could be answered, last." Feeling his patient stirring, he knew that he might soon be able to obtain verbal information and hoped it would be forthcoming.

A low groan left the man and his eyes opened. For a few seconds, they stared upwards blankly and Doc waited in tense expectancy. Then the glassiness left them. Giving another pain-filled moan, the man stared around and started to move.

"Norrie!" the woman gasped, but Lynn kept a firm hold of her.

"Take it easy, *amigo*," Doc advised gently, restraining the man's attempt to sit up and look around. "Your lady's safe and hasn't been hurt. But you have. Not real bad, but enough to stop you jumping up and doing a jig."

"Hey!" wailed the wounded outlaw, still holding his shoulder. "Hey, doctor. I've been shot—"

"I'd never have guessed," the Texan snorted, without looking around

"You—You've got to—!" the outlaw yelped and tried to shove himself up from where he was sitting.

"Stay put there, bucko!" commanded the bank guard, taking his attention briefly from the second outlaw who was also seated and holding his head with both hands. "I reckon the doc'll get to you when he's finished with that gent."

Agony and weakness had brought about what Doc required, rather than a desire to be compliant. What was more, Lynn had eased the woman around until the injured man was able to see her. Giving something that was between a groan and a sigh of relief, he relaxed.

"That's some better," Doc drawled. "Can you see all right?"

"Yes," the man replied, but there was an edge of doubt in his voice.

"Don't try to show us how tough you are," Doc warned. "If your eyes aren't right, tell me so."

"I can see all right," the man insisted. "Except that my head hurts."

"That's to be expected," Doc said calmly. "It doesn't tell me anything—"

"What about?" the man gasped, beginning to move again.

"Anything I don't know," Doc replied, still in calm and soothing tones. "So just sit nice and easy. You've been hit at the side of the head by a bullet, which it could have been a whole heap worse. As far as I can tell, you've got nothing more than a bad graze across the side of the head. It'll need stitching and I can't do that here, not having anything to work with. So I'll just bandage it and see about getting you somewhere that it can be done."

"I thought—!" the man began, but the words died away as there was a disturbance at the door.

"Shucks, way you're jumping around and taking on, there's nothing bad wrong," Doc declared cheerfully and looked at the three men whose entrance had brought the patient's words to an end. "Howdy, Sherry."

"I thought it was *you* I saw outside," Phillipe St. Andre stated, glancing around the room. "What happened?"

Dressed in much the same manner, with the exception of their footwear, and matching Doc in height, the Captain of Detectives was a handsome man with curly black hair and a neatly trimmed moustache. His wide shoulders and slender waist suggested great strength and physical fitness. For all his aristocratic upbringing, he had a reputation for being exceptionally efficient at his work and real tough when the need arose.

"Those yahoos thought they was the James and Younger boys," Lynn explained. "They figured on robbing the bank."

"That's what an informer came in and told me," St. Andre admitted, throwing a smile at the girl. "So I gathered some help and came to stop them."

"You got here a mite too late," Lynn stated. "We couldn't wait."

"Did you catch the two who took the greaser stand-off?" Doc inquired.

"Huh?" said the puzzled Captain.

"The two's ran out on their *amigos*," Lynn translated, wondering why her husband was showing so much interest in the pair. "A couple of your boys were headed after them when I fetched Doc in here to do something more useful."

"They waited for us when they saw us coming," St. Andre explained. "I sent the men I brought with them after the escapees. How is that gentleman, Doc?"

"He's not too badly hurt," the Texan replied. "I'll put a bandage around his head and then I want him taken either to a doctor, or to the Hospital, whichever's nearest, so he can be attended to better than I can manage here."

"I'll have it done," St. Andre promised, turning his gaze to a man who was coming into the building.

"They'd gone from sight when we went through the alley, sir," the newcomer reported. "Lieutenant Redon's got men asking around if anybody's seen 'em and others going along the streets. But if they once get down towards the river—"

"Finding them won't be easy," St. Andre finished for the detective, then he looked across the room. "Will you attend to that wounded man when you've finished with this gentleman, Doc?"

"You can count on it," the Texan answered, wondering if he could persuade the injured outlaw to give him information that would help to locate the man who had had the two Colt Pocket Pistols.

Doc wanted to know how the weapons had come into the young outlaw's possession and, if Hayden Paul Lindrick was still alive, where he could be found. The Texan had a score to settle with the original owner of the Colts.

CHAPTER FOUR

It'll Hurt Less If You Talk

Pompous though he might look and act, the manager of the New Orleans' branch of the First National Bank proved to be a man of some forethought. Seeing what was going to be needed, he—not without an expression of extreme relief—handed the three revolvers to Captain Phillipe St. Andre and scuttled into his private office behind the counter. On his return, he was carrying a small bowl filled with water and a wooden box which held the other items Doc Leroy would need for the temporary treatment of the wounded man's head. Nodding his gratitude, the Texan set to work bathing the graze and then began to affix one of the bandages from the box.

"We came prepared for trouble," St. Andre remarked, watching Doc's slim and almost boneless seeming hands moving with such deft assurance. He found himself remembering how swiftly they had drawn and fired the ivory handled Colt Civilian Model Peacemaker during the demonstration. "But we didn't expect to arrive and find that you pair of wild cowboys had been shooting up everything in sight."

"Seemed like a right smart thing to be doing at the time," Lynn Leroy put in. "And, happen you figure I'm a cowboy, it's time I had a long talk to Alice about you."

"I stand corrected, *cherie*," St. Andre declared, favouring the girl with a bow and employing the French word which, in its corrupted Americanized form had given him his nickname.

34

Then he glanced from the two wounded outlaws to their dead companion. "Hum! I wonder what the *Intelligencer* will have to say about *this*?"

"Tell them it was the owlhoots who did all the shooting, only they were mighty poor shots," Doc suggested, having seen examples of the kind of distorted reporting which appeared in the very "liberal" *New Orleans Intelligencer* when the police or anybody else in authority were concerned. Then an idea came to him and he went on, "Those kind-hearted soft-shells[1] who write for it won't be any too pleased about you leaving that poor hurt *hombre* over there to suffer, for shame. You get him taken in a back room some place and I'll 'tend to him."

"Can't you treat his wound where he is?" St. Andre inquired.

"Nope, not the way it has to be done," Doc stated, with such a definite air that his wife and the detective looked at him. Glancing at the outlaw, who was staring at them, he called, "You-all don't mind if I take you in back someplace and work on you, now do you, *hombre*?"

"No!" the man moaned. "Only come and do something for me. I'm bleeding real bad."

"Just what's on that tricky Texas mind of yours, Doc?" Lynn inquired, beating St. Andre to the question; although he had intended wording it somewhat differently.

"Nothing more than wanting to do the best I can for that poor hurt gent, honey," the Texan replied and, if his demeanour was any guide, butter would have had a difficult time melting in his mouth. "Which all these sober and upright, tax-paying members of the community have heard him say he doesn't mind it being done my way."

"Very well," the detective sighed, his curiosity aroused and making him willing to co-operate. He turned to the manager, saying, "Can we use your private office, Mr. Duprez?"

"I—" the official began, then saw St. Andre's brows knit in an unpleasant frown. He remembered that the other was not only a senior member of the New Orleans Police Department but belonged to a very wealthy and influential family who had

1. Soft-shell: a "liberal" with extremely radical views.

connections with the bank. "Er—of course you can, Captain."

Helping the groaning criminal to his feet, St. Andre's two detectives hustled him across the room. They left his handcuffed companion sitting on the floor under the watchful gaze of the bank guard. Having completed his work on the robbers' victim, Doc straightened up.

"Is—!" the woman gasped, moving away from Lynn who was taking her vanity bag and money from one of the tellers. "Will he—?"

"I've done all I can, ma'am," Doc answered reassuringly. "Now Captain St. Andre will have you both taken somewhere, so that the wound can be treated more adequately than I can manage with what I've got on hand. You can do that, huh, Sherry?"

"Of course," the captain confirmed and called to one of the uniformed officers who were keeping the growing crowd away from the bank's door. "Take this lady and gentleman to the Hospital in the paddy wagon, O'Reilly."

Waiting until the man and woman were leaving, Doc turned to go towards the manager's private office. On the point of following, Lynn asked St. Andre for her Thunderer. Taking out the weapon, having thrust it and the Pocket Pistols into his pockets, he handed it over. Tucking it into the vanity bag, she accompanied him as he went after her husband.

Like the detective, Lynn had no idea of what might be causing Doc to behave in such a fashion. However, even more than St. Andre, she could sense that he was deeply perturbed by something. It was, she suspected, linked to the pair of fine looking Colt revolvers which had been dropped by the fleeing outlaw. Restraining her interest, knowing that at least part of the answers might soon be forthcoming, she preceded the detective in following her husband through the door of the manager's office.

"Don't you reckon those boys of yours should go and make sure that other jasper stays put and can't escape, Sherry?" Doc remarked, indicating the plainclothes officers with what some people would have taken for a casual gesture.

"Very well," St. Andre replied, as he could not be counted

in their number, giving a nod of approval to his sub-ordinates. He did not know why the Texan had made the suggestion, but was convinced that there was a sound reason for it. Waiting until the pair had left, he anticipated a further request by closing the door. "Now what?"

"Now I can start work," Doc answered, in the same flat and unemotional tones that had aroused his wife's and the detective's suspicions. Turning towards the outlaw, who was slumped on a chair by the manager's desk, he continued. "I'm going to have to take off your clothes to get at that wound, *hombre*."

"Y-Yes—?" the man groaned and the Texan was pleased with the fright he showed at the prospect.

"Yes sir," Doc went on, exhibiting a relish that looked very convincing and saw the other's fear growing more intense. "It's going to be painful as hell. Fact being, I don't reckon you've ever felt anything hurt so bad."

"Wha—Wha—?" the man croaked, sinking even lower on the chair.

Listening, Lynn and St. Andre exchanged puzzled glances. They knew it was anything but sound medical policy to emphasize how much a proposed treatment would hurt. Nor did they doubt that Doc was equally, even more, aware of the fact. Certainly it was doing nothing to calm the patient.

"Shucks, ain't no point in hiding the truth from you," Doc declared, advancing with what the wounded man imagined to be an air of eager pleasure at the prospect at starting such painful work. "Tell you, though, it'll hurt less if you talk."

"T—!" the outlaw gasped. "Talk?"

"Why sure," Doc agreed. "Tell us a few little things to take your mind off the pain. Like what kind of liquor you drink. Who your favourite girl is—*Or where those two butt-dragging yahoos who ran out on you-all might have gone*."

"Huh?" grunted the outlaw, having noticed and drawn the correct conclusions from the way the sentence following the brief, dramatic pause had been spoken. "You want—?"

"I don't *want* anything, except to help you forget how I'm going to have to hurt you and to get started afore you bleed to death," Doc interrupted. "Shucks, it's not like they stood by you all loyal and true after that *loco* son-of-a-bitch started all the fussing. Why, as soon as they saw things were going wrong, they just up and took to running, leaving you to face all the blame."

A faint smile of enlightenment came and went from St. Andre's face as he realized what the Texan was hoping to achieve. There was a chance that the two outlaws would evade their pursuers and the information, if it was obtained could help to locate them. However, he was too experienced a peace officer to offer any comment. He felt sure that they would learn more if he remained in the background and allowed his companion to extract the answer.

"You—I—!" the outlaw spluttered, fortunately without looking at the detective and asking for official intervention.

"Look at it this way," Doc drawled, taking a flat leather wallet from his coat's inside pocket. "I'm a mighty strange *hombre*. When I want something and don't get it, I kind of forget things. Like now. Damned if I haven't forgotten I've got this knife with me. So I'll have to tear your clothes away instead of being able to cut them off."

"D-Don't forget what happened last ti—!" Lynn began, stepping forward with an attitude of well-simulated alarm.

"Shut your damned mouth, woman!" Doc blared, swinging around and showing none of the delight he was experiencing over his wife's intervention.

"Ye—Yes—husband!" Lynn replied, backing away as if afraid of the anger she had caused to be diverted upon her. "Only the last time—."

"You mind your own affairs, woman!" Doc snarled and turned his gaze to the now terrified criminal. "Now which is it, *hombre*, are you going to talk all soothing to me while I work?"

"Th-They got away?" the man asked.

"Would I be wasting my damned time if they hadn't?" Doc spat back and made as if to return the wallet. "Oh well, let's start by hauling off that cloak—"

"You'll maybe find them at Coffee Dan's!" the outlaw decided hurriedly, after a moment's thought and staring at the sadistic features of the man into whose hands he had placed himself. "Yeah! That's where they'll go to. Tick's Coffee Dan's nephew and that Blaby son-of-a-bitch's never been anywhere else."

"Coffee Dan's, huh?" Doc repeated, in tones redolent of disbelief, despite having thrown a quick look at St. Andre and received a nod which told him such a place existed. "Now you're *right* sure of that?"

"Hell, I don't know for sure!" the outlaw practically sobbed. "It's the likeliest place for Tick and Blaby to head for. Even without Dan being Tick's uncle, ain't neither of them over smart. They're not likely to know anywheres else to go and hide out. It's where we was supposed to meet up again if anything happened and we got separated."

"Doctor!" St. Andre barked, deciding that they would be unlikely to learn any more through the present means. "I can't have *this*. Either take care of the prisoner, or I'll have somebody fetched who will."

"All right, all right!" Doc grumbled. "I'll start. Here, women, take my case and I'll get to ripping off his clothes. He might be lying and I'd hate like—"

"Honest, Cap'n," the outlaw wailed, becoming aware of St. Andre's presence and feeling relieved. In spite of the lies which were published by the *New Orleans Intelligencer*, it was generally accepted among the criminal class of the city that, while tough, St. Andre was fair and did not sanction the mistreatment of prisoners. "I've told this feller all I know. If you don't catch those two yellow bellied sons-of-bitches afore, you'll be likely to find 'em at Coffee Dan's."

"I believe you," the detective declared, truthfully, deciding the man was too terrified to lie. "Start work on him, doctor. And do it properly. *Cut* the clothing away."

"Why sure," Doc assented sullenly, knowing better than to make a change in his behaviour that would let the outlaw find out a trick had been played. Opening the wallet, he took out a sturdy scalpel. "It's not everybody's are so damned soft hearted where lousy thieves are concerned."

Displaying a surprising delicacy, considering his callous attitude up to that point, the Texan started to slit first along the cloak-coat's shoulder seam so as to remove its sleeve. At first, the outlaw was wary and frightened. Then he saw the change in his tormentor and attributed it to St. Andre's opportune "arrival" and presence.

Calling on Lynn for help, Doc continued to work. Still slitting with the scalpel, he removed the jacket's and shirt's sleeve until he had exposed the man's shoulder. Granted his first clear view of the wound, he felt relieved to find that he had been correct in his assumption with regard to it.

When ignited by a spark of flame from the percussion cap, either as a separate item or when built into the metal base of a cartridge, the black powder charge burned to form a vast volume of gas. This in turn served to drive the bullet forward. In a weapon such as the type of Colt Thunderer used by Lynn, complete consumption of the powder had not been attained before the lead emerged from the two and a half inch long barrel. So there was a noticeable loss of thrust as the gases were able to disperse on leaving the muzzle instead of being compelled to expand along the metal tube.

Even at so short a range, the Thunderer's .41 bullet had suffered a sufficient loss of velocity that needing to cut a passage into the thick cloak-coat and other garments had prevented it from going right through the bulky man's shoulder. While it had been painful and—particularly as it had been delivered by a beautiful young woman—unexpected, the wound was far less serious than would have resulted from a weapon which made a fuller utilization of its propellant charge.

Having had an extensive acquaintance with injuries that had resulted from gun-shots, Doc had of necessity studied their effects. Drawing on his knowledge, he had been satisfied that the man would not bleed to death, or even be as badly hurt as he had obviously imagined. To give the Texan his due, if he had felt that the other's life might be endangered, he would not have delayed in starting the treatment. As it was, he had played on the outlaw's state of shock and fear of being seriously injured to obtain the information he required.

Now, as a result of his stratagem, Doc had at least a starting point in his search for the man who had been in possession of Den Lindrick's two Cold Pocket Pistols. He also knew that he would have difficulty in accomplishing anything further without help. He did not know the city well enough and had no official status. Neither would have stopped him from trying if he had not been sure that he could obtain assistance.

There was, however, the matter of the wounded outlaw demanding Doc's attention. While he had no sympathy for the man and considered that the injury had been well deserved, he was no sadist. Having done what he set out to achieve, he was willing to devote all his skill to the task in hand. For all that, he knew under the circumstances the aid he could render was limited. In addition, more capable—or, at least, better equipped—assistance was readily available."

"H-How bad is it?" the outlaw begged.

"Well now," Doc replied. "I've seen worse plenty of times and the fellers who had them pulled through. Happen you've *got* to get shot, this'll do until a bad one comes along."

"What can you do for him?" St. Andre asked.

"That depends," Doc replied, opening the box which the manager had brought from the office and had carried back.

"On what?" the detective inquired, wondering if he might have misjudged the Texan's character and the display had not merely been a pose to fool their captive.

"It's this way, feller," Doc told the outlaw, losing his earlier hectoring aura and ceasing to call the robber by the hard sounding "*hombre*". "Your wound's nearly stopped bleeding and that means no major blood vessel, vein or artery, has been touched. But the bullet's in there, along with pieces from your cloak-coat, jacket and shirt. They'll have to come out."

"Th—Then get them—!" the wounded man began.

"I done it before and could again," Doc admitted, his voice still gentle. "Except that I've only got a couple of scalpels and a probe with me. Happen you're taken to a hospital, they'll have everything on hand to clean it out a damned sight easier and less painful."

"P-Painful?" the outlaw repeated, throwing an alarmed glance at St. Andre.

"They can put you to sleep there, so you'll feel nothing and it'll all be over when you wake," Doc elaborated. "There's only two ways I can do it and neither're easy. I can whomp you on the head and work while you're unconscious. Only it's difficult to hit just hard enough and not *too* hard. Or I can have you held down and put something in your mouth for you to bite on while I'm working."

"Isn't there any other way?" St. Andre put in.

"It's one or the other," Doc stated, directing his answer to the outlaw. "I'll bandage you so that you'll not lose any more blood, or be hurt any worse while you're going to hospital. Or I can work right here."

"C-Can you get me there, Cap'n?" the man asked. "I won't give you any trouble, or try to get away, if you do."

"I'll have a cab called to take you," the detective promised and looked around as the door opened.

"Hey, Cap'n," one of the plain-clothes officers said, stepping into the room. "We've got trouble."

"What kind?" St. Andre asked.

"Mudgins from the *Intelligencer*'s outside," the officer replied, his tones showing how he regarded the newspaper reporter. "He's demanding to be let in and find out what's happened."

"I'll come out," St. Andre decided.

Working as efficiently as when he had dealt with the gang's victim, after the detectives had taken leave of them, Doc bandaged the outlaw's shoulder and fastened the arm in a sling. Then, telling his patient to stay put, he escorted Lynn from the office. They found that the reporter from the *Intelligencer* had been allowed to enter. Tall, lean, with untidy long hair, he had a sallow, thin and sullen face with deep set eyes. He had on a red necktie and his good quality suit, like the grubby white shirt, looked dishevelled from choice rather than any more valid cause.

"Is that some of your *police* work, Andre?" Mudgins was demanding, deliberately leaving out the prefix to the detective's name, as he pointed at the corpse.

"I killed him," Doc announced, walking forward and becoming aware that his wife was no longer accompanying him.

"You?" Mudgins snorted, swinging around to look the Texan over from head to foot.

"Me," Doc confirmed.

"Why?"

"Considering he was fixing to shoot *me*, it seemed like a mighty reasonable thing to do."

On the point of calling the tall young man before him a liar, Mudgins thought better of it. There was something disconcerting in the other's coldly challenging gaze. What was more, if he should be speaking the truth and, in his heart, the reporter did not doubt it, he would be likely to take grave exception to such a suggestion.

"How do you feel about your officers allowing men to walk the streets armed, Andre?" Mudgins challenged, deciding to pick on a safer target.

"If you mean the criminals," the detective answered. "No law *anybody* can make will stop them going armed."

"I meant this man!" Mudgins corrected, indicating Doc.

"Now hold hard there, *hombre*!" the Texan barked, before St. Andre could comment. "I'm no damned criminal, so I obeyed the law of your city and wasn't toting a gun. I took it off one of the gang and used it on another who was figuring on killing me with that scatter *he* was breaking the law by carrying."

"But if you'd been able to disarm one of them," Mudgins protested, his newspaper being stout advocates for legislation that would make the ownership of firearms illegal and, like all of his bigoted kind, he hated to be reminded of the fact that only law-abiding people would heed such a ruling. "Why did you have to kill him?"

"Look up there," Doc suggested, pointing to the two holes which had been shattered in the ceiling by the shotgun's loads. "I was here and he was where he's lying. Getting shot at with something capable of doing *that* might not seem like much to you, *hombre*, but it scares seven shades of shit out of me. Fact being, I get kind of touchy when it's likely to happen."

"Who are you?" Mudgins requested, wishing he had the courage to put the question as a demand.

"The name's Marvin Eldridge Leroy," Doc replied, hoping the other had not heard of him in connection with his peace officer activities in Arizona.

"Are you a policeman?" the reporter inquired.

"Nope. I'm a student at the Soniat Memorial-Mercy Hospital," Doc answered, then turned towards the detective. "I've fixed up that outlaw's wound like *you* told me to, Captain *St. Andre*. Now you can have him moved to hospital."

"Thank you," St. Andre replied. "And, if you'll excuse me, Mr. Mudgins, I think *you've* delayed me long enough from having the man moved. So I'll go and attend to it."

Rage distorted the reporter's unprepossessing features as the detective and the Texan walked away. He had the kind of mentality which glorified bad manners, but not when they were directed at him.

Muttering to himself, the reporter turned his attention to the bank's employees and Lynn. The stories given to him by the former tallied with what Doc had already told him and offered no way of being turned against the police. Nor were the girl's efforts any more fruitful. A good actress, she left no doubt that her husband—without identifying him as such—had acted in the only way possible to avert a massacre of everybody in the bank. Nor did the wounded outlaw improve matters, as he declared he had received good treatment at St. Andre's hands and claimed his dead companion was a notorious wanted killer from out West.

It was a bitter and furious Mudgins who stalked from the building. He swore that somebody would pay for the disrespect with which he had been treated. There was no way he could strike at St. Andre. So he decided that he would do everything in his power to ruin the damned medical student's chances of becoming a qualified doctor. Considering how to bring this about, he went in search of a cab to take him to his newspaper's office.

CHAPTER FIVE

He's From West of the Big Muddy

"All right, Doc," Captain Phillipe St. Andre said, as he accompanied the young couple from the New Orleans' branch of the First National Bank. "What was all that in the manager's office about?"

"You've got to admit that, even for *you*, you was acting just a little mite peculiar, husband of mine," Lynn Leroy went on. "Sure, I know that you'd like to see *all* of those yahoos tossed in the pokey. Which's what they've asked for and deserve, not counting honest folks being safer if they are. Only, happen I know you, there's a whole heap more to it than that."

"There is," Doc Leroy confirmed quietly, although he was pleased to think that he appeared to have achieved one other purpose while in the bank. He had turned the attention of the *New Orleans Intelligencer*'s reporter away from the peace officers and had personally accepted responsiblity for the death of the outlaw. Now, he realized, the time had come for him to explain why he had taken the steps which had produced some possibly useful information. In view of a report received by the detective, the latter might prove useful. "Only I'd rather not talk about it standing here."

Half an hour had elapsed since the attempted hold up and all the on the spot formalities had been completed. While the injured outlaw was being taken to have his wound cared for, his unhurt companion was questioned and supported his sug-

45

gestions as to where the two who had escaped would probably go to seek a hiding place. The dead man had been removed and, when it returned, the paddy-wagon was used to take the prisoner into custody. However, as yet, Blaby and Tick had evaded capture and the hunt in the area was continuing. However, acceding to Doc's request without questioning it, St. Andre had not sent officers to Coffee Dan's.

A reporter from the city's other newspaper, the *New Orleans Picayune* had arrived, but was a vastly different proposition from the *Intelligencer*'s representative. All he had wanted was the facts and did not attempt to find ways to blame anybody except the would-be robbers for the fate that had descended upon them.

Finally, after Lynn had deposited her money, St. Andre was taking the opportunity to satisfy his curiosity over Doc's behaviour.

"There's a coffee house along the street," the detective remarked. "We could go there and let *Lynn* buy us a meal, seeing she's so affluent, while we talk."

"I've a better idea," Doc contradicted, darting a glance at his wife. "Why don't we let her get us a cab ride to our place. It'll save time and we can talk on the way."

"I'm for that," St. Andre smiled.

"*I'm* not," Lynn declared. "About *me* paying, I mean."

"You're out of luck, honey," Doc pointed out. "The voting's two to one in favour of *you* paying."

"So I have to, huh?" Lynn asked.

"That's the way it goes in a democracy," St. Andre pointed out, smiling as he compared Doc's wife with the Western girl who had been responsible for his nickname. They were very much alike, Lynn Leroy and Miss Martha Jane Canary,[1] high spirited, unconventional, exceptionally capable of taking care of themselves even in the unfamiliar surroundings of a bigger city than either of them had ever seen before coming East, and with a similar sense of humour. "So I'm afraid that you must pay, *cherie*."

1. Some details of Miss Martha Jane Canary's career and capabilities can be read in the *Calamity Jane* series. J.T.E.

"Like hell you're 'afraid,'" Lynn scoffed, then gave a piercing whistle to attract the attention of a passing *vis-à-vis*[2] cab's driver. As he was reining his two-horse team to a stop, she went on, "All you pair're afraid of is that I *won't* pay."

Helping the girl aboard and allowing Doc to climb in, St. Andre followed them. Once the driver had been given his instructions and the vehicle was moving, Lynn and the detective looked expectantly at the Texan.

"I reckon I told you why I didn't get to be a doctor years back, honey?" Doc inquired.

"Why sure," the girl replied. "Your folks were killed in a feud back to Lampasas and you couldn't make it."

"That was part of it," Doc admitted and there was a hardness underlying his quiet words. Although he had gradually succeeded in putting from his mind the idea of seeking out the man responsible for the killing he was finding that to have his loss recalled still aroused a sense of great bitterness. "I was wanting to find the man who had caused it to happen."

"You know him?" St. Andre put in, from the seat with his back to the driver.

"I knew him," Doc confirmed. "His name's Hayden Paul Lindrick, a *pistolero valiente*—a hired gun hand—and *real* good. So good that he reckoned he didn't need anything heavier than the matched brace of fancy Colt Pocket Pistols he always toted."

"You mean like those two that yahoo dropped when he lit out from the bank?" Lynn guessed, having identified the kind of weapons she had been handed by her husband and noticed their excellent condition.

"More than that, honey," Doc corrected and, for all his drawl, he was as tense as a tightly stretched steel spring. "They *are* them."

"Do you mean that you *recognized* them?" St. Andre ejaculated, taking the two revolvers from his jacket's pocket. After looking at them for a moment, he raised his eyes and went on, "Are you certain?"

"They've been rechambered, but the rest is just as I re-

2. *Vis-à-Vis*: a carriage with the passengers' seats facing each other.

member them," Doc declared with quiet conviction and explained how he had come to his conclusions regarding the
ownership of the weapons.

"Much of what you say is true," St. Andre conceded, turning the revolvers in his hands and studying the initials carved
on the ivory butts. "But I think I'm right in assuming that it
wasn't the man Lindrick who got away?"

"It wasn't," Doc agreed. "He was a whole lot younger and
Lindrick wasn't in the bank or I'd have recognized him, even
if he didn't me."

"There was only one Westerner among them and you killed
him," St. Andre replied. "All the others I saw and, from what
was said, the one they call "Tick," were homegrown thieves."

"Not Blaby," Doc objected. "The way he talked and acted,
he was from west of the Big Muddy like the *hombre* I put
down."

"No further east than Arkansas," Lynn seconded. "And I
wouldn't say he's a goober-grabber,[3] but closer to Texas."

"*North* Texas," Doc corrected.

"Do you think that Lindrick's in New Orleans?" St. Andre
asked, being willing to accept his more experienced companions' opinions on the outlaws who had come from the West.

"I don't know," Doc answered thoughtfully. "In the days
when I knew him, Lindrick was a gun hand, but not thief. Of
course, I've heard nothing about him for a fair spell. Could be
he's changed his name, and had to because he'd gone owlhoot
and was wanted."

"He could be dead," Lynn pointed out. "Happen, like you
said, he was so took by those two 'shoat-legs' to get them
rechambered, *he* wouldn't be likely to have sold or let them
go without real good cause."

"Like if they had been taken from him after his death?" St.
Andre suggested.

"One thing's for sure," Doc drawled. "That yahoo who ran
out wasn't good enough to have taken them from Den Lindrick if he's anywhere near as fast as he used to be. And he
wouldn't be so old now, not more than forty."

3. Goober-grabber: derogatory name for a native of Arkansas State.

"Jack McCall wouldn't have lived out two seconds happen he'd been stood in front of Wild Bill when the 'deadman's hand' was dealt in Deadwood,[4]" Lynn reminded her husband. "Speed only works if you're given a chance to use it."

"I'm not gainsaying that, honey," Doc said soothingly.

"Anyways," the girl went on, eyeing her husband in the partly speculative and partly, *"You* aren't fooling *me"* way he had come to know and love. "One feller who can likely tell us the answers isn't too far away."

"He isn't," the Texan concurred.

"Only, you being just a half smart lil country boy in the big city and all, you conclude that you might need help to find him."

"A smart man knows his limitations," St. Andre remarked, guessing where the comments were leading to.

"I don't see what *that's* got to do with anything's we're talking about," Lynn protested, looking from one to the other of her companions in a pointed manner. "But I reckon, husband of mine, that you figure's how you'd likely get along better with somebody who knows the range riding point for you."

"I'm not too proud to take good advice," Doc conceded.

"Who said anything about *good* advice?" Lynn demanded.

"If this is leading up to what I've a terrible feeling it might be," St. Andre said, directing his words at the Texan and pointedly ignoring the girl. "There's only one thing I don't understand."

"What's that?" Doc inquired.

"Why aren't we going straight to Coffee Dan's instead of by way of your place?" the detective asked.

"For two reasons," Doc explained. "First off, Lynn's fixed up to meet Alice there."

4. Jack McCall shot James Butler "Wild Bill" Hickok in the back as he was playing poker at the Number 10 Saloon in Deadwood, South Dakota, on August 2nd, 1876. The hand Hickok was playing at the time of his death was two pairs—ace and eight of clubs and ace and eight of spades —which subsequently became known as the "deadman's hand." Hickok makes a "guest appearance" in the "The Scout" episode of: *Under the Stars and Bars.*

"I'm buying her dinner out of the reward," the girl supplemented. "Was figuring it'd be for four, but to do that, we'll likely have to wait a while."

"Secondly," Doc continued, as if his wife had not spoken. "I want to get dressed before I go calling."

"Which means you want to go and collect a gun," St. Andre stated, remembering how he had heard Calamity Jane employ a similar expression.

"You can bet your sweet Louisiana life I do," Doc agreed. "From the way that *hombre* talked and you know it, I don't reckon that Coffee Dan is used to law abiding folks who'll obey the law by *not* toting a gun. And, any time I'm going some place like that, I figure I've as much right to be carrying one as they have. Fact being, what happened at the bank proves I'm right. Next time, I might not get the chance to lay hands on one."

"Very well," St. Andre sighed, nothing in his attitude showing that he went along with the Texan's line of reasoning. He was aware that the only kind of customers who knowingly frequented Coffee Dan's were criminals and they were not likely to adhere to the Civic Ordinances which—in the case of the law-abiding citizens—prohibited the carrying of firearms within the city limits. However, he was also cognizant of the fact that the *Intelligencer* would react strongly if they learned that a private citizen had done so with his approval. "It's a pity you're not still an Arizona Ranger, Doc."

"How come?" Lynn asked.

"If I was a visiting peace officer from out West and hunting for a wanted owlhoot," Doc explained. "I'd be allowed to tote a gun like the local john laws."

"That's true," St. Andre confirmed.

"Would that apply to a deputy sheriff of Two Forks County, Utah Territory?" Lynn asked, with such an aura of disarming innocence that the two men exchanged glances.

"It would," St. Andre admitted, showing relief. "You never said that you were a deputy sheriff, Doc."

"He *isn't*," Lynn admitted. "Thing being, the sheriff back there's such a blasted liar that, was anybody from down this way to send and ask, I'd just bet he'd say 'yes' like it was true."

"Now that's no way to talk about your brother-in-law, lil wife," Doc protested, although he knew she was correct in how Waco would respond if such a request for confirmation was received. "Even if his missus did lick you in a fist fight."

"Lick *me*!" Lynn almost screeched and spread her hands in a gesture of resignation as she turned her gaze to the detective. "Why, Sherry, it took Sister Beth all her time and a lot of puffing and panting to even hold me to a stand-off."

"Very well, *Deputy Sheriff* Leroy, of Two Forks County, Utah Territory," St. Andre said, with an air of solemnity that he was far from feeling. "Do I take it that, in your official capacity, you are requesting the co-operation of the New Orleans Police Department to apprehend a possible fugitive from justice who is wanted by your office?"

"Nope," Doc denied and held down the grin which struggled to rise as he heard his wife's gasp and saw the detective show a similar astonishment. "What I'm *requesting* is help in arresting a man who I was witness to escaping from a bank hold up."

"Here in New Orleans?" St. Andre practically gasped, knowing that their argument would be weakened by that fact.

"Happen *anybody* thinks to ask where, then I'd have to say 'yes,'" Doc replied. "But only *if* I'm asked. You see, I'm not like that shiftless brother-in-law of mine. I'm a *right* truthful young feller."

"Lord!" Lynn yelped, raising her eyes and a hand towards the ceiling of the *vis-à-vis*. "Don't let lightning strike this poor, worthless sinner. He's only joshing."

"*He* missed His chance," the detective sighed, then stiffened to adopt a parody of the Chief of Police's attitude when dealing with an official matter. "Very well, *Deputy Sheriff* Leroy. As Captain of Detectives, I'm only too pleased to offer you every assistance in this matter of law enforcement that you have brought to my attention. And may *le Bon Dieu* have mercy on my soul."

The rest of the journey went by uneventfully, apart from the two men planning their campaign for the visit to Coffee

Dan's. It was decided that they would call at Police Headquarters on their way, in case the two outlaws they wanted had been captured in the vicinity of the bank. As far as the rest went, they made only a general arrangement, knowing that circumstances might make them deviate from it.

On reaching the apartment building in which the Leroys were making their temporary home, it was in a pleasant part of the city's middle rent district, the party found Alice St. Andre waiting. Small, petite, beautiful and tastefully dressed, she sensed that something untoward had happened as soon as she saw their faces when they alighted from the *vis-à-vis*. However, she had sufficient self control to restrain her curiosity until they were inside Lynn's and Doc's suite of furnished rooms.

For all that she had the upbringing to be expected from a daughter belonging to a very wealthy Southern family, Alice had accepted that marriage to a peace officer had its unpleasant and unpalatable features. Furthermore, she showed no revulsion on hearing of the part played by Lynn in preventing the robbery. Having ascertained that the girl was suffering no ill effects, she sat back and listened to the rest of the story.

"Of course you have to help Doc!" Alice stated firmly, after her husband had mentioned their intentions. "The only pity is that you have to think up a reason for doing it. How long will it take?"

"There's no way of knowing, *cherie*," St. Andre apologized, having taken and kissed Alice's hand in gratitude for her support. "If he's been captured, we'll be back as soon as we've talked to him. But going to Coffee Dan's will almost certainly take much longer."

"I wouldn't wait dinner for us," Doc went on. "But, happen you'd like to give us fifty dollars or so, Lynn, we'll pick up a bite when we're through."

"I'm not *quite* sure what you mean, dear." Alice lied, smiling rather than blushing over the blunt and forthright response Lynn had made to the suggestion. She had heard similar terms employed by stablehands and others when they were unaware of her presence. "But I'm in agreement with it."

"Looks like we'll have to buy our own dinners, Sherry,"

Doc sighed. "I'll be with you as soon as I've changed clothes and got dressed."

"What's wrong with the clothes you're wearing?" Alice inquired.

"For one thing, this here's my best Sunday-go-to-town suit," Doc replied. "For another, except for good ole Bat Masterson,[5] I've never yet seen a real, genuine Western peace officer dressed this fancy. Third reason being that Lynn'd whomp me good was I to get these clothes mussed up."

"Why can't *you* be so considerate, Sherry?" Alice demanded with mock severity.

"I think I'll come with you while you get changed, Doc," St. Andre suggested, in tones of martyrdom.

Stripping off his jacket as he walked, the Texan led the way into the bedroom. He dropped it on the bed and opened the wardrobe. Inside, among the other clothes, hung the attire which he felt was best suited for his needs. Carrying his selection to the bed, he placed the clothes on it. Reaching underneath with his foot he pulled out a metal bootjack in the shape of a cricket.[6] Hooking the back of his left boot into the jack's horns, he placed the other foot on its body. Doing so allowed him to lever off the tight, yet comfortable footwear. Reversing the process, he removed what would otherwise have been an obstacle to changing his pants.

With a low grunt of relief and satisfaction, Doc discarded the vest, tie, stiff collar, shirt and the suit's trousers. In their place, he donned a dark blue flannel shirt with an attached collar that he did not fasten and a tight rolled, multi-coloured bandana. These were augmented by a well washed pair of Levi's trousers whose legs had cuffs three inches wide and were left outside the boots he returned to his feet.

Before taking his dressing any further, the Texan returned to the wardrobe. Kneeling, he unlocked and opened a small

5. William Barclay "Bat" Masterson: among other things, a deputy town marshal in Dodge City, Kansas and noted as a dandy dresser. Makes a "guest appearance" in: *Trail Boss*.
6. Cricket: *Gryllus Domesticus*; a leaping orthopterus insect with long antennae and six legs. Something like a grasshopper in appearance.

trunk. St. Andre sucked in a breath, but did not speak, when he saw what was being taken out.

Unrolling the brown gunbelt, which still had bullets in its loops, the Texan buckled it around his waist. Settling it in position, he tied the thongs attached to the bottom of the contoured and carefully designed holster about his right thigh. Then he unrolled his ivory handled Colt Civilian Model Peacemaker, which had been stored wrapped in a piece of soft cloth. Setting the hammer at half cock and opening the loading gate, he turned the cylinder. As each chamber's rear end was exposed, he inserted a fat .45 cartridge from the box he had produced with the rest of his gun fighting equipment. Having done this six times, he dropped the revolver into its form-fitting holster.

"I don't reckon I'll take old Betsy along," Doc remarked, indicating the Winchester Model of 1876 "Centennial" rifle that was in the wardrobe, as he closed the trunk. Hanging up his suit, he drew on the brown coat—its right side stitched back to allow clear access to the Colt—which went with his present attire. "Seeing's how you're loaded for bear, I shouldn't need it."

"I didn't know it showed!" St. Andre said indignantly, glancing downwards.

"It wouldn't to city folks," Doc replied soothingly. "But us Westerners grow up learning to watch out for things like that."

"Huh!" St. Andre sniffed, pulling aside the left flap of his coat to expose a Merwin & Hulbert Army Pocket revolver held in the retaining springs of a shoulder holster. "I thought having it under my arm, nobody would notice it."

"Like I said," Doc consoled. "I learned real early the things to look for. Let's get going."

Returning to the dining-room, the men said their good-byes to their respective wives. There was no time for more talk. On dismissing the *vis-à-vis*, St. Andre had asked its driver to return and Lynn had seen it outside. Taking his black Stetson, to replace the bowler he had hung on the rack alongside it on his arrival, Doc set it at the traditional "jack-deuce" angle over his right eye.

Accompanying the detective from the apartment house, the

Texan's face showed nothing of his feelings. However, he was eager to set out on a mission which might help him find the man who had been responsible for his parents' death. In spite of that, he was satisfied with another matter. If there should be gun play during their quest, he had arranged for an excuse his companion could use to deal with any repercussions from the *New Orleans Intelligencer*.

CHAPTER SIX

If You Touch It, You're Dead

Coffee Dan's did not appear to be dispensing any of the beverage implied by its proprietor's name. Nor had the sale of such a commodity in its liquid form ever been a major part of his revenue. In fact, the title had arisen because he had founded his fortune during the War Between The States by making coffee beans a major portion of every cargo his ship had run through the United States' Navy's blockade of Southron ports.

It seemed to Doc Leroy, as he stepped through the front door at eight o'clock in the evening, that but for a few obvious changes, he might have been entering a saloon in the toughest section of any large Western town. The decor was different, tending to have to do with riverboating rather than ranching, mining, buffalo hunting or whatever else was the industry carried out by the local clientele, and while the attire of the customers was more suitable to working on a paddle-steamer, or doing manual labour connected with the river front, the employees might have belonged to any cow town. That particularly applied to the heavily made up and garishly, somewhat daringly, dressed women who were mingling with the crowd.

If the Texan found his surroundings of interest, the people in the room were regarding him with an equal curiosity. Cold eyes in vicious, sullen and brutal faces were taking in every detail of his appearance. There was an almost universal response to the sight of his armament. First a glance in passing,

56

then the gaze would snap back and fix on his low tied Colt. In a Western saloon, no matter in what type of activity the clientele found employment, the ivory handled Peacemaker and its well designed rig would have been the first thing to be noticed. Having looked him over, many of his examiners turned their attention pointedly to one particular section of the long bar counter.

Following the direction of such a scrutiny, Doc had no difficulty in deciding at whom it was being turned. Standing clear of the hard-worked bartenders and in a position which offered him an excellent point of vantage to keep an eye on them or the other occupants of the room, was a man who must be the owner. The Texan would have identified him without having had him described and pointed out by Captain Phillipe St. Andre.

On visiting the headquarters of the New Orleans Police Department, Doc and St. Andre had learned that the two outlaws were still at liberty. So the detective had changed into suitable attire which was kept in his office and collected three of his men who were dressed in a similar fashion. They had accompanied the Texan to the vicinity of Coffee Dan's, but stayed outside. Although St. Andre had come as far as the building and indicated its owner through a window to his companion, he and his men had seen the difficulties that would accrue if they followed Doc in. Their garb had been sufficient of a disguise to let them pass through the dark streets without attracting unwanted attention, but they could not have hoped to enter the well illuminated interior of the saloon without being identified, if not personally, for what they really were. Instead, they were lurking across the street ready to dash over at the first sign of a disturbance.

Although it had been many years since Coffee Dan had given up life at sea, he still sported the peaked hat and frock coat favoured by captains of merchant ships. In his early fifties, he was a medium sized man who gave the impression of being as broad as he was long. A scar ran up his left cheek, disappearing under the black patch that covered his near eye, giving his tanned face a savage and sinister expression.

Even as Doc's eyes reached the owner, Coffee Dan gave a

backwards jerk with his head. Nor did the Texan have any doubt as to whom the signal was intended. Watching the room to his rear with the aid of the long mirror behind the bar, he noticed two large and burly men move from where they had been leaning against the wall on either side of the main entrance. Slouching forward, they were starting to converge upon him.

"Hi there, cowboy!" a good looking and shapely woman greeted, walking over and reaching out with her hands as if to add to the warmth of her welcome. Her accent was that of a Kansan, but her friendly smile did not extend as far as her eyes. Rather they were wary, like a wild animal approaching something dangerous and poised for flight. "You're a long ways from your home range."

"Likely, ma'am," Doc conceded in a hard voice, preventing her from taking hold of his *right* arm. "And anybody's hails from the Jayhawker State should ought to know better'n try a thing like *that*. You go keep them two *hombres* who're dogging my trail company and tell 'em why they shouldn't."

"I wasn—!" the woman began, taking a hurried step away, but showing no resentment at hearing what had been her home State referred to with the derogatory name given to it by Southrons.[1]

An uneasy silence fell over the room and all activities came to an end. Patrons and employees alike watched the Texan continuing his progress towards where Coffee Dan was standing behind the bar.

Still keeping the two brawny roughnecks under observation via the mirror, Doc strode on without letting his interest in them become obvious. He moved with a steady, almost feline-like step. All the time, his right hand dangled in a deceptively casual looseness that tended to emphasize it was in close proximity to the butt of a Colt carried in a holster which had been

---

1. During the War Between the States, the Jayhawkers of Kansas were bands of irregulars who—like the Confederate States' guerillas of William Clarke Quantrell, William "Bloody Bill" Anderson and George Todd's ilk—used patriotism as an excuse for arson, looting, pillage and other atrocities.

designed to facilitate the *very* rapid withdrawal of the weapon. Everything about him conveyed the impression and suggestion of a latent, deadly, yet completely controlled menace. It was the posture of a man who realized he was treading dangerous ground, but felt confident that he could deal with any threat which might be presented.

All in all, it was a masterly performance.

Yet attaining it was not difficult.

Throughout most of his life, Doc had been in contact with the kind of man he was purporting to be. So he was able to give an almost faultless impersonation of a genuine bad *hombre*, as opposed to a swaggering blow-hard show off trying to act like one. Perhaps the full subtlety of his performance was lost upon the majority of his audience, but he considered that he was being successful among that portion of his watchers with whom he was most directly concerned.

Throwing a glance at Coffee Dan, the saloongirl made a worried gesture. Then she turned towards the two roughnecks. Although her back was to the Texan, he guessed that she was delivering his warning. One at least did not require advice. He was already displaying a perturbed aspect which suggested he had had contact with Western gun fighters and knew just how fast and deadly such a person could be.

Much to Doc's satisfaction and relief, although neither emotion showed on his pallid features, Coffee Dan obviously respected the woman's judgment. He gave a quick and perceptible prohibitive shake of his head which caused the two roughnecks to come to an immediate halt. The gesture was repeated to the owner's left and right, being directed at two equally large and tough looking men who were standing one at each end of the counter.

In spite of the restrictions being placed upon the bouncers by his employer, the largest and head bartender reached under the counter with both hands.

"I don't know what you've got down there, *hombre*," Doc remarked, in an almost casual tone—yet which also held a note of menace—looking straight at the bartender and then swinging his gaze in a marked fashion towards Coffee Dan. "But I'd leave it, was I you. Happen it's what I reckon, afore you could bring it up, I'd have killed *somebody*."

Reading the intended message from the quietly spoken yet plainly heard words that sounded in the stillness of the room, the saloonkeeper felt as if a cold hand had touched him. A well travelled man, he had seen Western gun fighters' deadly techniques demonstrated while on a visit to the Texas seaport of Corpus Christi shortly after the War. Furthermore, he was currently—or had been, if the reports of how the robbery at the First National Bank had ended in disaster were correct— acting as host to a capable exponent of the draw-fast-and-shoot art. So he did not doubt that the threat could be carried out. Nor was he under the slightest misapprehension as to the identity of the "*somebody*" to whom the newcomer was refer-ring.

"Avast there, ye lubber!" Coffee Dan bellowed, as if hail-ing the maintop in the teeth of a gale, glaring at his employee until the hands were brought empty into view. Then he re-turned his gaze to the Texan and forced a smile. "No offence, me hearty, only it's not usual we have a matey come aboard armed for boarding."

"Happen that means what I figure. I'd's soon leave off wearing my pants as this old hog-leg," Doc drawled, indicat-ing the Colt with a brief gesture and came to a halt at the counter in front of the saloonkeeper. "My *bueno amigo* Big Hadle's a mite the same way."

"*Big Hadle?*" Coffee Dan repeated, contriving to intro-duce a note of innocent interrogation into his voice as if he had never heard the name. For all that, he could not prevent his eyes from flickering briefly to the stairs which led to the accommodation on the building's upper floor. "I can't say's how I recollect your shipmate."

"Now that's right strange," Doc replied, refraining from duplicating the other's involuntary action despite having drawn certain deductions from it. "Because the word I picked up was for me to meet him *here*."

"No offence again, me hearty," Coffee Dan stated, his tones now registering puzzlement. "But at which post office would ye have collected his signal?"

"Likely, being a honest and God-fearing gent and all,

you've never heard of it," Doc replied. "But it's the one run
by young Hobart Turtle, for his pappy Ram, up around Wi-
chita Falls way."

Even as he was supplying the information, the Texan could
see that his gamble was paying off. While the two captured
bank robbers had told him the name of their leader, he had
deduced from hearing Big Hadle's accent that the outlaw came
from North Texas. So he had mentioned a family which had
long been prominent in the annals of Texas law breaking.[2]

"Huh huh!" Coffee Dan grunted non-committally, but his
attitude had undergone a subtle and, to Doc, satisfying
change.

"Don't say 'no offence' again," the Texan requested, fore-
stalling the other's intended utterance. Glancing over his
shoulder, he went on, "Is it *always* this quiet in here?"

"What-ho, me hearties!" Coffee Dan boomed out, in a way
that combined joviality with a command, taking the newcomer's hint and glaring around the silent room. "Why the
doldrums? Whistle for a wind, somebody, before we're all
becalmed and die of thirst."

Being aware of what their employer was demanding, the
saloon's employees resumed their activities and set about
stimulating the customers' interest in the interrupted pastimes
of drinking and gambling. Soon the hubbub of talk, laughter,
shouts and the clinking of glasses welled up to the volume that
it had been before Doc's entrance. For all that, more than one
person darted glances at him. However, none displayed too
great curiosity or attempted to approach. They knew their host
too well for that.

"You can talk as safe now as if we had the quarterdeck to
ourselves, me hearty," Coffee Dan announced, after his purpose had been achieved. Then he slapped his hand on the
counter. "Shiver me timbers, here's a fine way to welcome a

2. Details of the Turtle family's participation in Texas law breaking are
given in: *Ole Devil and the Caplocks, Set Texas Back On Her Feet* and,
by inference, *The Quest for Bowie's Blade*, and *Mr. J.G. Reeder, Meet
'Cap' Fog!* J.T.E.

shipmate. Would you do me the honour of splicing the main-brace?"

"What'd that be?" Doc inquired, being as puzzled by the nautical jargon as the saloonkeeper would have been if listening to a cowhand employing the special terms of his work.

"A drink, me hearty."

"Just so long as it *isn't* coffee."

"Bring aft the rum for me shipmate and me, ye lubber!" Coffee Dan commanded with a grin. After the head bartender had placed two glasses filled with a dark liquid in front of them and withdrawn, he went on, "Was your shipmate offering to find you a comfortable berth along of him, bucko?"

"Allowed we should sort of go into the banking business together," Doc replied, making a correct deduction about the meaning of the question. "Said there was some right smart opportunities for a man with my qualifications down here."

"Drink hearty, bucko," Coffee Dan requested, raising his glass. "I don't know how to tell you this, but you've got here too late."

"How's that?" Doc demanded, having copied his host's action but setting the glass down with the liquor untasted and scowling as he felt would be expected of him.

"He set sail without you," Coffee Dan obliged. "Went to take aboard a cargo, but struck a reef and foundered."

"Talk English, damn it!" Doc snarled, getting the gist of what he was being told and reacting as the kind of person he was pretending to be would when hearing such news.

"Your shipmate and his crew tried to rob the First National Bank," the saloonkeeper elaborated. "Only they fell afoul of a whole boarding party of Pink-Eyes.[3] There was some shooting and your shipmate was laid low and's gone aloft for the last time." A frown came to his face and he eyed the Texan speculatively. "Haven't you heard about it? I thought it was been talked about all over the city."

"It could be for all I know," Doc replied, having anticipated such a question and obtained information which he

3. Pink-Eye: derogatory name for an operative of the Pinkerton National Detective Agency.

hoped would counter it. "I only just now come in on the *Louisiana Lady*, asked how to find your place and come straight on down here."

"Then it's not likely you'd have heard," Coffee Dan conceded, being conversant with the Mississippi River's traffic and knowing the steamboat *Louisiana Lady* had arrived from the north earlier that evening.

"Maybe *you'd* oblige me by telling about it?" Doc suggested.

"There's not much I can te——," the saloonkeeper warned. Glancing to the left, a frown knit at his brow and he went on more than a little irritably, as if he did not approve of what he had seen, "There's a matey in the offing who can set you a better course than me over what happened."

Following the direction of the other's gaze, Doc stiffened slightly as he saw the two young men who had escaped during the robbery. They were walking down the stairs side by side and so absorbed in a conversation that neither had any attention for what was going on around them. Their condition of ignorance continued until after they had reached the floor of the bar-room. In fact, they had turned and approached to within fifteen feet of where Doc was standing before they became aware of his presence.

Of the two, Tick showed the least reaction on finding that they were confronted by the grim faced Texan. Not only did he fail to identify Doc as the cause of their misfortunes, he was confident that he was safe in his uncle's premises.

"How the hell did you fi——?" Blaby gasped, coming to a halt with his face losing most of its colour and displaying alarm.

In spite of the nature of the unfinished question, Doc felt that it had not been invoked by recognition of him as being responsible for the disastrous failure of the bank robbery. Judging by the reaction Blaby knew *what* rather than *who* he was.

An expression of near panic played on the young outlaw's features. His right hand made as if to move in the direction of the old walnut handled Colt Cavalry Peacemaker which was thrust into the waistband of his trousers so its butt showed prominently from under the left side of his jacket. It looked to have received far less car and attention than the two revolvers he had discarded in his flight.

"Don't," Doc advised quietly. "If you touch it, you're dead!"

Soft spoken though the words had been, they produced an instant effect. Running the tip of his tongue across lips that had suddenly turned very dry, Blaby stood as if he was turned to stone.

Once again, although the crowd lacked the experience a similar group of Westerners would have had with such a situation, silence dropped on the room.

As the saloonkeeper had claimed, the story of the abortive bank hold up was fairly common knowledge. Many of the customers and all of the employees were aware of Tick's relationship with Coffee Dan and of the company he had been keeping recently. So, from what they had heard and deduced regarding the events of the afternoon, most could guess he had taken part in the unsuccessful robbery. They were less able to decide upon Doc's status and involvement. However, they could see that Blaby—who they all felt sure had been another active participant—was deeply alarmed by the sight of the Texan.

More than one customer, who had no desire to be found by the police on premises where there had been a shooting, cast glances about them in search of the nearest means by which they could take a rapid departure. However, having no wish to draw attention to themselves, even those who were already standing made no attempt to leave.

"Why howdy there, Blaby-boy. Damned if I figured's how I'd find you *this* easy."

The words, in a hard mid-Western accent, seemed far louder than their actual volume in the newly dropped silence. They were spoken by a man who had come through the main entrance and was crossing the floor without attracting the attention he would have done if the crowd had not been otherwise engaged.

Turning his gaze to study the speaker, Doc could read the

signs from what he saw as if they were painted in scarlet letters ten feet high.

So could Blaby!

If the young outlaw's gasp of horror and the way he staggered—with his hand falling limply to his side—to crouch against the bar was any indication, he knew why the man had come in search of him.

It was clearly for no friendly purpose!

Close to six foot tall, lean, tanned and hard-featured, the newcomer emerging from among the crowd wore garments which suggested they had been purchased far to the west of the Big Muddy. He had on a dark grey Stetson creased with a Dakota full curl pencil roll,[4] which caused the front of the crown to be higher than the rear. Long fringed and open, his buckskin jacket was decorated by red, white and blue Indian-style patterning. Unlike Doc's, which was rolled tightly and fastened at the side of the throat, his red bandana had only been folded once to form a triangle and was knotted behind his neck. His double-breasted dark blue shirt had the tag of a tobacco sack dangling from its right pocket. Somewhat newer than the Texan's, his Levi's pants were tucked into low heeled and square toed boots of a kind no cowhand worth his salt would consider wearing.

Although obviously a man of the West, the newcomer had no gunbelt about his waist. Doc knew that such an omission was the exception rather than the rule. What was more, a bulge beneath the right side of the jacket—detectable to the Texan's trained gaze—suggested that he did not lack a weapon.

Because of the number of people between them, the man had not noticed Doc and believed Blaby's behaviour had been produced by seeing him. As he passed the forefront of the onlookers, he realized that he had been in error. Swinging his gaze from the cowering outlaw to the Texan, he came to a halt.

Slowly, as Doc turned from the bar, the newcomer looked

---

4. Full curl pencil roll: where the brim's edge is curled all the way round and dips deeply at the front and back.

him over from head to foot and, with eyes as experienced as his own, paid *great* attention to the hang of the gunbelt carrying the ivory handled Colt.

Completing his scrutiny, the man raised his eyes to the Texan's pallid face and they held a challenging glint.

"Well I'll be damned and double damned!" the newcomer declared, having formed an accurate estimate from what he had seen. That was the rig of a master gun hand and, if his deductions were not at fault, its owner was capable of utilizing it to its full and deadly potential. "Blaby-boy, I knowed's how good old Haynes Lashricker set a whole heap of store in those two fancy lil guns of his'n you wide-looped. But he never let on that he was fixing to send more'n one of us to look for you."

CHAPTER SEVEN

He's *Mine* and I'm Taking Him!

"Please, Mr. Royster—mister—!" Blaby wailed, looking from the newcomer to Doc Leroy and back, as the Texan was realizing the implication of the Westerner's words. "I—I—I— don't have 'em any more!"

"Now that's what I'd call right unlucky for *you*," the newcomer declared, but his attention was directed at Doc rather than Blaby. "Seeing's how I've a fair notion of what to do, that being the case."

"Well now, *hombre*," the Texan put in quietly, reading the challenge in the newcomer's statement. "There's some might say's how you've got here a mite too late to do anything."

"Belay there, me hearties!" Coffee Dan boomed out, keeping his hands in plain view and flat on the top of the bar. "As captain of this vessel, I'd like to know what's what. Are ye Pink-Eyes, or officers of the law?"

Intelligent and well-educated, his over-use of nautical expressions had become an ingrained habit and was appreciated by wealthy visitors who came on what would one day be referred to as "slumming" expeditions, the saloonkeeper realized that he had been tricked by the first of the Westerners who had arrived. The implied friendship with Big Hadle was a lie. Blaby's response to the sight of the tall, pallid faced stranger was evidence of that.

All of which raised the point of what had brought the two

men of the West to Coffee Dan's. According to Blaby and
Tick, on their return earlier that evening, the rest of the gang
had been killed and there was no way anybody could find out
where they were seeking refuge. Yet the arrival of the Westerners suggested that two persons at least had made the discovery.

As yet, all of the newcomers' attention had been directed at
Blaby, but Coffee Dan had his nephew's welfare and safety to
consider. It had not been with his consent that Tick had joined
the abortive robbery, but—faced with a *fait accompli*—family ties dictated he did all he could to ensure the young fool
did not suffer the consequences of such ill-advised behaviour.
He and his companion were supposed to have remained concealed in the upstairs room until arrangements could be made
to get them out of New Orleans, but they had failed to do so.
Nothing could change that, but the saloonkeeper felt he should
make his position in the affair plain before it went any further.

"I don't know about this feller," the man called Royster
answered, indicating Doc with a jerk of his head, "But I'm
neither."

"Or me," the Texan admitted. "And *I'm* not interested in
your nephew."

"*You* don't want to arrest young Tick here?" Coffee Dan
asked, looking at Royster.

"I've just come for that butt-dragging yahoo Blaby is all,"
the Westerner stated, evading what he sensed could have been
a trap laid by the cold-eyed son of the Lone Star State.

"So you don't want *my* nephew?" Coffee Dan asked.

"*I* don't!" Doc asserted quickly.

"He don't mean nothing to *me*," Royster went on an instant
later, guessing that to do so would affect his chances favour-
ably. "All I'm after is Blaby there. He's *mine* and *I'm* taking
him."

"Well now," Doc drawled, being aware that the second part
of the Westerner's speech had been directed as much at him as
at the saloonkeeper. "I've always been told it's good for a
man's soul to want, but not to get what he's wanting."

"Now *I* wouldn't know about that," Royster countered,
reading just as much defiance in the Texan's statement as there

had been in his own words. "Seeing's how I've never wanted *anything* and let *anybody* stop me getting it."

"Like they say," Doc answered, in the same even and emotionless tones he had employed throughout his conversation with the other Westerner. "There's always a first time for *everything*."

Watching and listening, Coffee Dan thought fast. His every instinct warned that it would be dangerous and possibly fatal to intervene. No coward, he was equally anything but a reckless fool. Faced with the kind of unpleasantness to which he was accustomed, he would have dealt with it unhesitatingly. However, he realized that the two men across the bar lived by rules and a code as alien as if they had come from another world. So, being a wise and cautious—within reasonable and sensible limits—man, he decided to let them settle their differences without obstruction on his part.

Much as Doc wanted to avoid trouble of the kind which he guessed was coming, having deduced the nature of the man with whom he was contending, he doubted whether it would be possible for him to do so. From what had been said, he could guess at Royster's reason for seeking Blaby out. Preventing the other from carrying out his purpose could, in the Texan's estimation, only be done in one way.

While a whistle, or a yell, would bring Captain Phillipe St. Andre and the other detectives on the run, Doc considered that was not the answer to his dilemma. Brave, tough and capable as they undoubtedly were in their own field, none of them had had experience in tackling a competent Western gun fighter. Unless Doc's judgment of such a matter was seriously at fault, Royster was all of that. Only another—and better—exponent of the *pistolero* arts could hope to go against and survive an encounter of that nature. So the Texan accepted that he must stand, or fall, on the strength of his own prowess rather than endanger the lives of his friends.

"Hey now!" the hired gun ejaculated, still staring straight into Doc's face. "I know you from someplace."

"Could be," Doc answered, conscious of the need to prevent his identity from being disclosed. "I was there one time, way back."

"I've never seen you around the Kenton spur," Royster continued and, for the first time showed puzzlement.

"That could be because I've never been there," Doc pointed out.

Despite the casual way in which he was speaking, the Texan felt a surge of excitement. He had heard something of the state of affairs that was developing around the town of Kenton on the border between the States of Colorado and Wyoming. The Union Pacific Railroad was putting a spur line through the region, but the right of way was being disputed. From the rumours which had been circulating before he had left Two Forks, hired guns, as so often happened in such cases, were flocking to the area in search of employment with one faction or the other.

In the old days, Hayden Paul Lindrick had made his living from similar states of affairs. Very efficient, intelligent, unscrupulous it was said, and a born leader, he had become the controller of the gun hands hired by the Maudlin family. Before that, if the stories which were circulated had been accurate, he had always served as the boss gun—being set over lesser lights, even *pistoleros* of Royster's calibre—wherever he had plied his deadly trade.

If the conversation to which Doc was a party had been any guide, Lindrick, although using a different name, was still following his profession and had not descended in status. He must be at—"

"And I'll tell you something else, *beef-head*," Royster growled, cutting through Doc's thoughts and employing the derogatory name for a Texan which had arisen through their State's dependence on the cattle industry for revenue.[1] "You can forget any notions you might have of going there with Haynes Lashricker's fancy guns to set you in good with the big boss."

1. It would be many years before "black gold," oil, became a major factor in the economy of Texas. How the cattle industry came to play such an important part in the growth of the Lone Star State, particularly in the impoverished years following the end of the War Between the States, is told in: *Goodnight's Dream*—American title *The Floating Outfit*—and *From Hide and Horn*. J.T.E.

"Strange you should mention that," Doc remarked, with a deceptively casual tone that did not fool the other Westerner. "Could be it's just what I have in mind."

"It is, huh?" Royster asked, his right hand moving in what was a significant manner anywhere west of the Mississippi River but for one thing.

"It could be," Doc repeated non-committally, wanting the first aggressive gesture to come from the other man.

"Well I'll be damned and double damned!" Royster ejaculated, as if suddenly recollecting something of importance. His right hand rubbed at the place on his off thigh where a correctly designed holster would hang. At the same time, moving in a casual appearing gesture, his left hand reached across as if to remove the sack of tobacco from his shirt pocket. "Mind if I roll me a smoke to steady my nerves, Texas. Damned if I wasn't forgetting that this ain't back home and I'm not toting a gun."

Even as Royster was speaking the last words, his left hand shot under the right side of the jacket with a sudden increase in the pace with which it had been moving. His fingers and thumb enfolded the butt of the Colt "Storekeeper's Model" Peacemaker[2] in his spring-retention shoulder holster. The move was made with such speed and precision that, taken with it being performed "southpaw," he considered that— even against a man of the Texan's quality—it should have had every chance of success.

Unfortunately for Royster, he was up against a man who could claim few superiors in the art of gun fighting.

Having been aware that the other was carrying a concealed weapon, Doc had drawn the correct conclusion about where it was positioned. So he had not been diverted or distracted by the actions of Royster's right hand.

At the first positively hostile gesture, the Texan responded instantaneously. His right hand made an almost sight defying flicker. To the watching people in the bar-room, very few of

2. Colt "Storekeeper's Model," a Peacemaker with a barrel of four inches or less and minus an ejection rod for removing empty cartridge cases from the cylinder. J.T.E.

whom had ever seen a highly trained Western *pistolero* in motion, it seemed that the ivory handled Colt had leapt from its holster and into his grasp. Before any of the onlookers could fully appreciate what was happening, held at waist level and aimed by instinctive alignment, it roared and belched out smoke tinged with the flame of the muzzle blast. The .45 bullet, passing through the rifling grooves of the four and three-quarter inch long barrel, was propelled into the centre of Royster's chest.

Struck an instant before his own weapon had reached a point from which it could endanger his assailant, shock and pain twisted at the hired gun's face. He was knocked backwards and, as he went sprawling supine on the floor, his revolver flew unfired from his grasp. That was fortunate for him. If he had retained his hold on it, the Texan would not have hesitated before shooting him a second time. With such a man as Royster, one could not take chances and survive to tell the tale.

Seeing his opportunity, Blaby flung himself from his crouching posture by the bar. Ignoring the Colt in his waistband, his only thought being to save himself from whoever emerged as the victor in the corpse and cartridge affair, he started to race across the room.

Instantly, the other occupants of Coffee Dan's—who had sat or stood like statues all through the confrontation between the two Western men—erupted into motion. Scattering in every direction, spurred by a mutual desire to flee from the scene of a shooting, they would have come between Doc and his quarry if he had contemplated using the Colt. However, he had no such intention.

On the point of starting to give chase, Doc remembered an earlier incident in the saloon. Looking around, he saw that the head bartender was repeating the attempt to produce whatever weapon was hidden beneath the counter. Doubting if a verbal warning would suffice on this occasion, the Texan swivelled and, cocking the Colt's hammer, threw it upwards to allow for more careful sighting than he had used when dealing with Royster.

With his hands closing about the sawed-off shotgun that

reposed on the shelf in front of his usual position, the bartender saw what was happening. So did his colleagues and they showed an equal alarm to that of his. Letting out yells and displaying a grasp of the situation worthy of workers in a Western saloon, they started to fling themselves downwards out of the line of fire.

Having no wish to injure the bartender if it could be avoided, Doc laid his aim accordingly. He watched with satisfaction the other men behind the counter disappearing and saw the consternation on the face of his intended target. Then the Colt crashed, sending its load where the Texan meant for it to go. Hearing the eerie "whap!" of the lead passing close over his head, to fly on and end its propulsion without danger to anybody in the side wall of the room, the head bartender gave a frightened yelp. Taking an involuntary stride to the rear, he tripped over the feet of a colleague and fell backwards. Although he released the shotgun, its hammers were not cocked and it clatted harmlessly to the floor.

Thumbing back the Colt's hammer without the need for conscious thought, Doc tossed a glance at the owner of the saloon. Coffee Dan was standing as he had ever since the Texan had entered, face hard and lips tight. However, as Doc's eyes turned towards him, he glanced away. Following the direction of his gaze, the Texan saw that Tick was following Blaby's example. However, where the Western outlaw was making for the front door, the owner's nephew was fleeing towards a side entrance.

"It's Blaby I want!" Doc stated.

Receiving a nod of acceptance, the Texan resumed his interrupted pursuit. Before he had taken half a dozen strides, his quarry was already plunging through the main entrance. Instead of running straight ahead, the outlaw made a sudden swerve and disappeared from Doc's range of vision. However, he heard Blaby yell in alarm and the noise was followed by a heavy thud.

Running onwards, Doc noticed the Kansan saloongirl, and she reminded him of another possible source of interference. However, the two bouncers flanking the open front door made no attempt to prevent his departure.

On leaving the building, Doc discovered what had caused Blaby's abrupt change of direction and the reason for the noises which had followed it. Finding himself confronted by one of the detectives, who had been sent by St. Andre to find out what was happening in the saloon, the outlaw had tried to dodge aside. Instead of succeeding, he had been tackled and brought down. Even as Doc arrived on the sidewalk, his captor had a knee rammed against his spine and his right arm was twisted painfully behind his back. Doc was pleased to observe that St. Andre and the two detectives were holding their revolvers, even though he did not believe there would be any need to use them. They had left their places of concealment across the street and were approaching on the run.

"The other one took off through the side door!" Doc announced, pointing with his Colt-filled hand in the appropriate direction. "Only you'll likely have trouble telling which way he's gone. He had plenty of company lighting a shuck on his trail."

"See if you can catch him!" St. Andre commanded and, after his two men swerved towards the end of the building, joined the Texan in front of it. "We got the one you wanted, anyway, Doc. What was all the shooting about?"

"I had to throw lead into that *hombre* who followed me in," the Texan explained, twirling the Colt back into its holster and accompanying the captain to the main entrance. "Then I tossed a shot to scare the barkeeper out of fetching up and cutting loose on me with a scattergun. At least, I reckon that's what it was."

"Damn it, this place is starting to be like Dodge City!" St. Andre ejaculated, knowing that his companion would not have started shooting if it could have been avoided. He glanced to where his remaining detective was hauling a sobbing Blaby upright. "Can you manage, sergeant?"

"I reckon I can, sir," the officer replied, shoving his captive against the wall and taking a set of handcuffs from his jacket's pocket. "Let's have your fists behind your back, bucko."

"Do you think you can make him talk now you've got

him?" St. Andre inquired, watching the detective manacle the outlaw.

"It shouldn't be too hard, spooked as he is," Doc guessed, then shrugged. "Anyways, I reckon I've already learned most of what I need to know."

By the time Doc and St. Andre entered the bar-room, every customer had gone. Full and partly empty glasses, spilled drinks, money and chips left on the various gambling tables told that their departures had been hurried. All around, saloongirls, waiters and bouncers stared either at the two men who were coming in, or at the weakly moving shape on the floor. Behind the counter, the bartenders were standing up cautiously and clearly ready to return to their place of concealment if there should be the need. Only Coffee Dan seemed unmoved by the events of the past few minutes. However, he showed signs of surprise and perturbation as he realized who was with the Texan.

"You don't need the revolver, Captain," Doc announced in a carrying voice. "The gent behind the bar wasn't to blame for anything that happened. He didn't even know his man was trying to get out that scattergun, or he'd've right quick stopped him."

"Very well, sheriff," St. Andre replied, wanting to establish the idea that his companion was a Western peace officer. Knowing why Doc had made the suggestion, he returned the Merwin & Hulbert Army Pocket revolver to the spring clips of his shoulder holster. "I'll not take any action against him."

"And another thing," the Texan went on, as they continued to walk towards the counter. "Happen your men don't catch his nephew, I wouldn't waste sweat on hunting too hard was I you. Way he lit out of the bank this afternoon, he's had a scare that'll stop him trying anything like that again."

"I'll bear it in mind," St. Andre promised and could see the relief Coffee Dan was experiencing over the conversation. Indicating the man on the floor, he asked, "Is he going to die?"

"I don't know," Doc admitted, kneeling at Royster's side. As he did so, a shudder ran through the man and his body went limp. "I was using town loads, but there wasn't time for any fancy shooting. Where's the nearest doctor?"

Like most other top notch gun fighters, Doc hand loaded much of his ammunition. He also followed the practice of responsible peace officers. As their need for a revolver would generally be at close quarters and probably with innocent by-standers around, they did not use a full twenty-eight grain powder charge. By reducing the propellant power, there was less danger of the bullet driving straight through its intended mark and hitting somebody who happened to be standing be-hind.

For all that, the Texan knew just how deadly a .45 calibre bullet could be even when delivered at less than its full veloc-ity. What was more, it would still be inside Royster's body.

"Old Doc Crocker's got an office along the street a ways," Coffee Dan answered.

"Send for him!" Doc commanded, taking Royster's right wrist between his thumb and forefinger. *"Pronto!"*

"He's not likely to be sober enough to work this late," Coffee Dan warned.

"Send somebody to see if he is, anyway," Doc ordered, feeling the weak pulse beat.

"Sergeant!" St. Andre barked, looking to where the detec-tive was bringing Blaby into the bar-room. "Go with one of these people and see if you can bring a doctor."

"Yo!" the sergeant responded, giving the traditional cavalry signification that he understood the order. "You get over to the captain, feller, and don't make no fuss for him."

"Sit there!" St. Andre growled, as Blaby approached with hanging head and shuffling feet, pointing to a table. When the order had been carried out, he turned his gaze to the Texan. "Is there anything we can do to make him more comfortable?"

"He's better off where he is until we know for sure just how bad he's hurt," Doc replied, studying the blood that was oozing from the right side of Royster's chest and visualizing the organs, veins and arteries in its vicinity. "There's often more damage caused by well-meaning folks trying to make a wounded man "comfortable" than if he'd been left where he fell."

"Hey, me hearty," Coffee Dan called, glancing at the glass

which the Texan had set down on the bar. "You never had your drink."

"I reckon I'll come and take it now," Doc declared, deciding that the saloon-keeper might be expressing gratitude for his comments on entering with St. Andre.

The Texan's summation proved to be correct. As he took the drink, Coffee Dan showed no hesitation about giving him information regarding Big Hadle. However, before much could be said, the sergeant and his guide returned with the doctor. One glance told Doc that the newcomer was in no fit state to deal with such a serious wound. However, an examination of Crocker's bag disclosed that it held all that was necessary for the task.

Five minutes later, as Doc set to work with the instruments which he had cleaned, he thought how ironic a situation he was engaged in. After having shot Royster, who would not have hesitated to kill him had an opportunity arisen, he was about to use all his skill in an attempt to save the other's life.

CHAPTER EIGHT

It's the End of Your Career

"Good morning, sir," Doc Leroy greeted, halting in the doorway. Although the message he had received via one of the Soniat Memorial-Mercy Hospital's porters had left him with no doubt of the answer, he went on. "Did you want to see me?"

No student, even one of the Texan's seniority and with a clear conscience, ever faced with equanimity the summons to visit the Dean of the Medical College in his large and somehow grimly forbidding office.

However, in Doc's case, the request—demand would be a more accurate term—to attend had not been entirely unexpected.

Bare-headed, otherwise dressed much as he had been when taking his wife on the fateful visit to the New Orleans' branch of the First National Bank, Doc had a long white jacket over his suit. He showed no signs of the strenuous events in which he had participated the previous day, but he suspected that they were responsible for the summons.

Watched by Captain Phillipe St. Andre, Coffee Dan and such of the saloonkeeper's employees who had had the stomach—or morbid curiosity—to witness the sight, the Texan had gone about the task of trying to save the life of the man who had tried to kill him. Being aware of how dangerous making the attempt might prove, he had decided against having Royster moved any more than was necessary. Instead, he had the floor alongside his patient covered with sheets of clean newspaper. Then, exercising extreme care, he had had the unconscious hired gun moved on to them. Even in the urgency of the moment, he had found the thought of the use to which he was putting the *New Orleans Intelligencer* was not without a certain piquancy. It was, in his opinion, one of the few useful purposes to which such a newspaper could be put.

There had been no time for Doc to waste on such levity. While a couple of Coffee Dan's saloongirls were trying to sober up Doctor Crocker, at St. Andre's instigation, the Texan had gone to work. Exposing the wound, by cutting away the intervening clothing, had been the easiest part of the operation. As was the case with the man who had been shot by Lynn Leroy's Colt Thunderer, the bullet had not gone straight through to emerge at the rear. However, Royster was hit in the chest cavity; a vastly more vulnerable region than the shoulder, particularly as the bullet had carried portions of the garments through which it had passed into the wound.

There had been an added complication for Doc to contend with!

By sheer bad fortune, the lead had struck the right breast pocket of Royster's shirt. Doing so had added fragments of the tobacco sack—which had been a part of his attempt to trick his victim, offering him an apparently innocent reason for his left hand to approach the concealed revolver—and some of its contents to the other debris inside his torso.

Very careful and delicate testing with a twelve inches long, slender blunt probe had located the bullet. To a man of Doc's experience, removing it with the aid of a pair of thin forceps —even though they were inferior to a set he had had designed to his own specifications for such a purpose, but did not have with him—had caused no difficulty.

Extracting the other foreign bodies had been another matter entirely.

Nor had Doc been entirely successful in doing so.

Manipulating the instruments with a feather light but deftly sure touch that under different circumstances—and with the thorough education in such matters he had received—might have turned him into a successful dishonest gambler,[1] Doc had felt for, found and drawn forth the small, bloody wad which formed the bulk of the problem. Pushed in ahead of the bullet, the pieces of buckskin, flannel and cotton from jacket, shirt and undershirt were together. The two slivers of thin muslin from the sack of Bull Durham[2] were among the other materials when he had separated them, but at least some shreds of the tobacco were almost certain to have been squeezed out of the container and entered the wound. Nor, in spite of his skill, with the limited resources he had available, could he hope to find and remove them all.

Crocker, having been forced to drink copious amounts of strong black coffee and doused with cold water, had recovered sufficiently to take notice while Doc was still working. However, although a qualified medical practitioner, he had not attempted to interfere. In fact, at the completion of the operation, he had complimented the Texan and stated he could not have handled the situation nearly as well. A similar sentiment was later to be uttered by the intern at the Sara-Mayo Hospital, to which Royster was taken, on examining the result of Doc's labours.

With the hired gun treated to the best of his ability and disposed of, Doc at last found himself free to concentrate upon the matter which had brought him to the saloon and which was once again uppermost in his thoughts. From the information he had been given by Coffee Dan and the still terrified young outlaw, he had learned enough to make him sure that the owner of the two Colt Pocket Pistols was Hayden Paul Lindrick who could be found at the town of Kenton on the Colorado-Wyoming Border. The saloon-keeper had known

1. Examples of Doc Leroy's manipulative dexterity with a deck of cards are given in Case Four "Set One, Catch One" of *Arizona Ranger*.
2. Bull Durham: one of the best known and most popular proprietary brands of smoking tobacco in the United States of America. Originally produced by John Ruffin Green, near Durham's Station, North Carolina, in 1865, William Blackwell took control over the Company after his death in 1869. It has been claimed by some authorities Green had based the now famous "standing bull" trademark from a similar illustration on the jars of Colman's mustard which was available in powder form at that time.

little beyond what he had been told by Big Hadle, that the man the two Westerners had known as Haynes Lashricker was acting as boss gun on the side of the Union Pacific Railroad and apparently ruled the members of his faction, which appeared to be gaining ascendancy, with an iron hand.

When questioned, showing a pathetic desire to behave in a co-operative manner, Blaby had at first tried to pretend he was given the two revolvers. Finding out that his captors were not particularly interested in how the weapons had come into his possession, he had described their owner. On hearing him mention that there was a scar in the shape of a flattened "W" running across "Lashricker's" forehead, all of the Texan's last lingering doubts had been removed.

As his father was otherwise engaged, it had been Doc who stitched the jagged wound that had caused the scar.

Having obtained the necessary corroboration, the Texan had found himself on the horns of a dilemma.

In fact, even after a night of thought and deliberation, Doc still had not settled the matter of what to do about his discovery.

During the bitter days immediately following the death of his parents, Doc had had much on his mind. In addition to putting off his departure to commence what would have been his formal medical education, so as to start straightening out his father's involved and far from satisfactory financial affairs, he had worked at finding out who was responsible for the killings. According to what he had learned, four men were to blame. Three of them had died, although only one at his hands, but the fourth and, by all accounts, the most culpable had evaded his attentions.

The result of Doc's inquiries had established that Lindrick was the man in question. As if wishing to supply the conclusive proof of his guilt, he had fled from Lampasas County— in spite of serving what was emerging as the victorious side in the range war—and, apparently, had quit Texas too.

Finding a pressing need to both earn a living and acquire sufficient money to pay off various debts incurred by his father had precluded any chance of Doc either embarking on his proposed education, or carrying out a deliberate quest for vengeance. Not that he had ever completely forgotten Lindrick and, particularly in the early days, he had been alert for news concerning his whereabouts. None had been forthcoming.

Strangely, considering Lindrick's prominence and the interest taken by people out West in the activities of men in his line of work, Doc had heard nothing of him all through the years that had followed. Certainly he had never been mentioned in connection with any of the numerous types of conflict which called for the services of specialists in his deadly trade.

Always a realist, Doc had gradually come to accept that Lindrick might be dead or otherwise beyond his reach. So he had never considered carrying out what was likely to prove a futile search for the hired killer. The memory of his parents' death had never completely left him, but he had not permitted himself to brood upon its cause.

Having learned where Lindrick could be found, Doc had felt a resurgence of the old bitterness and anger. Yet he knew all too well how his situation had changed since the days when the incident occurred. Then he was a footloose drifter, with no other responsibilities than to earn sufficient money to clear off his father's debts. He had had nobody except himself to consider whatever he chose to do. Now he was a married man and on the threshold of the career he had so long desired.

All too well Doc appreciated the problems of confronting him. Within six months, perhaps less, he could take the qualifying examination that would entitle him to the title "Doctor of Medicine". Then he would be free to return West. He had already decided that he would set up his practice in Two Forks, Utah Territory, but visiting the town of Kenton would not take him too far out of his way when he left the trans-continental railroad.

However, in six months—or even less, depending upon how successful the Union Pacific Railroad were in establishing their right of way—Lindrick could have moved on. Men in his profession could not be hired cheaply. Nor, once they had served their purpose, did their employees care to retain them as reminders of the measures which had been employed to bring victory. So there was no assurance that he would be at Kenton by the time the Texan could reach the town. On the

other hand, to set off sooner could mean that Doc would have
to give up his hopes of becoming a qualified doctor.

Sensing his friend's dilemma, St. Andre had not carried out
a protracted investigation into Coffee Dan's connection with
the attempted bank robbery. While he had suspected that the
saloonkeeper was aware that it would take place, he knew
proving the point would be practically impossible. So there
had been no reason for them to linger. Leaving his sergeant to
deliver Blaby to Police Headquarters, the captain had accompanied the Texan to the restaurant where Lynn had taken Alice
St. Andrew and them out to dinner.

Not until Doc and his wife were alone in their apartment
had he told her of the latest developments and his dilemma.
Guessing at his inner turmoil, Lynn had not attempted to influence him one way or the other. She had stated that whatever he decided was all right with her.

For all his wife's support, Doc had spent a somewhat restless night. Nor had he reached any conclusions by the time he
had risen that morning. In fact, the matter was nowhere near
settled when he had left for the hospital.

On his arrival at the College, Doc found that his activities
of the previous day were public knowledge. The first thing to
greet him on his entrance at the student's lecture room, deliberately he suspected, had been the sight of the glaring head-
lines on the front page of the *New Orleans Intelligencer*.

"MEDICAL STUDENT INVOLVED IN DOUBLE
SHOOTING!"

Accepting the copy of the newspaper and reading the story,
Doc discovered that the reporter had done more than cover
what had happened at the bank. In some way, he had found
out about the incident at Coffee Dan's saloon. With an eye on
the possibility of a law suit for libel—but mainly due to fear
of the Texan's proven ability and proficiency in the use of
lethal weapons—Mudgins had toned down the calumnies it
had been his original intention to submit for publication. Instead, he had stated most—but not all—of the facts he had
gathered, naming Doc and the Hospital, with no more than the
usual near distortions his kind always employed when dealing

with a person who refused to subscribe blindly and fully to their lofty ideals.

On turning to it, Doc had found the newspaper's editorial column to be an impassioned declaim on the propriety of allowing a man to become a qualified doctor who was willing to kill other human beings, as they put it "in what passes as the interests of 'justice.'"

While studying the content of the editorial, Doc had guessed that there would be repercussions.

Confronted by two junior students, whose disdain for personal hygiene proclaimed their "liberal" pretensions, the Texan had listened to their demands that he state his views on "the moral ethics of one person considering he had the right to take another's life." He had answered in a way that left no doubt where he stood on the matter of a law abiding citizen's right to defend himself against thieves—even to the extent of killing—when the porter had delivered the message from the Dean. Leaving his interrogators to be mocked by their more sensible colleagues, he had come to answer the summons.

The Dean of the Medical College looked at the Texan from behind a desk upon which lay two newspapers. The upper, hiding the other, was a copy of the *Intelligencer* with its headline showing. "Come in and sit down, please."

Few people who came into contact with Doctor Alphonse Jules Dumoulin could have guessed from his present appearance that, in the days of his youth, he had led a wild and reckless life which had almost ended in an unnecessary duel.[3]

Of slightly more than medium height, always faultlessly— fussily even—dressed in the peak of a fashion permissible for a man of his years, the Dean of the College exuded an aura of conservative and conventional behaviour. The passage of time had added weight to his frame, but not to the extent of corpulence. What little hair remained was snowy white. Yet his still handsome face retained more than a suggestion of strength of will and his eyes showed something of their earlier restless fire.

Unlike many of his contemporaries, he had accepted over

3. Told in: *Ole Devil at San Jacinto*.

the past few years that his hands were not as steady as in the days when he had been building and maintaining his well deserved reputation as a surgeon *par excellence*. Now he did not take an active part in the performance of operations. However, as Doc was all too aware, he was still a powerful and influential factor in medical and surgical affairs in the city and throughout the State of Louisiana, as well as in matters that concerned that Soniat Memorial-Mercy Hospital and its Medical College.

To the students under him, as Dean of the College, Doctor Dumoulin was the epitomy of authority and wielded a decisive control over their hopes for the future. Intolerant of idleness and incompetence, he also had a reputation for being a stickler where the regulations governing their deportment and behaviour were concerned. For all that, there were vague rumours of how he had on occasion acted as a shield when high spirits had brought willing and capable students into conflict with their superiors.

Being older and more mature than all but a few of his classmates, Doc also had a young wife with whom to spend his leisure hours. So he had little contact with the activities of the students outside the College. Nor had he done anything inside that could have brought him before the Dean for disciplinary purposes since his arrival.

"I suppose you've seen *this*?" Dumoulin commenced, more as a statement than a question, waving a hand at the upper newspaper after the Texan had taken a seat and was facing him across the desk.

"Yes, sir," Doc admitted. "I don't buy the *Intelligencer*, but I've had it brought to my attention."

"So have I," Dumoulin grunted and repeated with a little more emphasis. "*So have I*. What have you to say about it?"

"It's true," Doc conceded. "As far as it goes."

"You did what it says?" the Dean challenged.

"Yes, sir," Doc replied, his voice flat, neither defiant nor apologetic. "I shot both of those men."

"Both?" Dumoulin said, showing slight relief. "Then you weren't involved in the incident at the saloon?"

"I was, sir."

"Then what do you mean, 'both'?"

"I killed the man at the bank, sir. But, although none of us mentioned it to the newspaperman, Lynn shot the other one."

"Mrs. Leroy?" Dumoulin barked and just a hint of an admiring smile came to his lips then disappeared just as quickly.

"She did it to save me, sir," Doc stated and explained the circumstances.

"I understand that you have served as a peace officer in the West?" Dumoulin remarked when the Texan had finished speaking.

"I was a deputy town marshal under Dusty Fog twice, sir, in Quiet Town and then later at Trail End,"[4] Doc confirmed. "Then I became a member of the Arizona Rangers."

"But you're no longer an officer of the law?" the Dean asked.

"No, sir. Nor have I said I was."

"But you've had experience with situations similar to that at the bank?"

"Not that close, but some."

"Enough for you to be convinced that they wouldn't stop with just one shooting?"

"I didn't *know* it for certain, sir," Doc admitted. "But it didn't seem like a good motion for me to stand waiting to find out before making my move."

"I'm not gainsaying *that*," Dumoulin declared.

Having delivered that sentiment, the Dean paused. Drumming his fingers on the top of the desk, he glanced from the slender young Texan to the two newspapers. The one underneath was that morning's edition of the *New Orleans Picayune*. It too carried the stories of the abortive bank robbery and the gun fight at the saloon. There was, however, a noticeable difference in the way the incidents were recorded. Although naming Marvin Eldridge Leroy as being involved in each occurrence, the *Picayune* claimed he was a peace officer from Texas and omitted all reference to his present occupation. They also included another piece of information which their rival newspaper had deliberately omitted.

4. Told in: *Quiet Town, The Small Texan* and *The Town Tamers*.

Considering the latter item, Dumoulin turned his gaze back to the Texan's pallid and composed face. The Dean was impressed and far from displeased by the other's demeanour. A lesser man in similar circumstances would have tried to use the fact that he had performed a difficult surgical feat under far from ideal conditions, thus saving the life of the man he had been compelled to shoot in self defense, as a reason why he should be excused from the consequences of behaviour which was not in accord with that expected from a student hoping to embrace the medical profession.

Such an idea had never entered Doc's head. He had read the *Picayune* while eating his breakfast at the apartment, and he guessed that a copy lay beneath the *Intelligencer*, as it was unlikely that the Dean would subscribe to the "liberal" newspaper. However, he had not envisaged that he would be facing the Dean over the matter. Nor, even now, did he consider that he needed to make any excuses for what he had been compelled to do.

In spite of the career upon which he was hoping to embark, Doc had no guilty feelings over shooting either man. A search of the wanted posters at the headquarters of the New Orleans Police Department had produced evidence that Big Hadle had murdered at least once in the commission of crimes. Royster had been a hired gun hand, selling his ability with firearms to the highest bidder, and had in all probability taken human life. Each had been prepared to throw lead into him if an opportunity to do so had been granted. So, as far as Doc was concerned, he had found himself in the ironic position of having to use his special knowledge to save the life of a man he had shot. He neither expected praise for the one, nor blame for the other.

For almost a minute, neither man spoke. It was Dumoulin who broke the silence.

"Nobody has the right to blame you for defending yourself and your wife, even to the extent of killing a thief who's threatening you," the Dean declared. "And it will be a sad state of affairs if the time comes when a man isn't allowed to do *that*."

"Yes, sir," Doc agreed and, remembering an incident Waco

had told him about,[5] went on, "Likely even a soft shell wouldn't object to having it happen should it have been them who've been threatened."

"I also have nothing but respect and admiration for any man who is willing to risk his life helping a policeman in an emergency," Dumoulin continued, without answering the comment. "But was there any need for you to go with young St. Andre to the saloon last night?"

"There was, sir," Doc said quietly, but with complete conviction.

"I hope that you have a *very* good reason," Dumoulin warned. "From the way the *Intelligencer* is carrying on, it's the end of your career they're after. And there are those, even on the Hospital's Management Committee, who will be sufficiently influenced by this muckraking garbage to support it."

"I'm sorry to have brought this on the Hospital, sir," Doc replied. "But I did have what I feel is a damned good reason for going to Coffee Dan's."

"Then tell me about it, please," ordered the Dean of the Medical College.

Starting at the beginning, Doc began to tell the full story. All the time he was speaking, he knew that his career hung in the balance and that he might have ruined his chance of becoming Marvin Eldridge Leroy, M.D.

Author's note: *The events in the next Chapters take place some ten years earlier than those recorded up to this point.*

5. Told in the "The Campaigner" episode of *Waco Rides In*.

PART TWO

Lil Doc and Sir John

CHAPTER NINE

That's Mean, Boy, *Real* Mean

Considering the state of affairs in Lampasas County, it might have been thought injudicious for Doctor Eldridge Jason Leroy, M.D. and his son, Marvin Eldridge—who had already by his eighteenth birthday acquired the sobriquet "Doc"[1] to have gone hunting along the Owl Fork of the river which had given their home County its name.

In some respects, like most of the problems which were besetting Texas in the summer of 1871, the feud between the Wensbury and Maudlin families, embroiling almost everybody else in the district, had its origins from the War Between the States. While Boone Wensbury and his sons—two of whom did not return—had ridden off to fight in the Army of the Confederate States, Taylor Maudlin had elected to keep all the members of his clan at home. There had been no suggestion of disloyalty to the South in the latter's decision. He had freely supplied cattle to help feed the Army of North Texas & Arkansas which, under the command of General Jackson Baines "Ole Devil" Hardin, C.S.A., had proved a serious thorn in the Union's side during the last two or so years of the conflict.[2] What was more, the

1. To avoid confusion, in the text of the following Chapters, the author will refer to Doc's father as "Leroy". J.T.E.
2. Details of General Hardin's participation in the Arkansas' Campaign are given in the author's *Civil War* series. J.T.E.

Maudlins had taken active part in the defense of their neighbours' properties against the depredations of marauding Indians and Mexicans while the other men were away fighting the Yankees.

Nobody in Lampasas County, probably not even the participants, could say exactly who or what provoked the feud in the first place. Certainly Maudlin's family were not entirely blameless. Equally, the fault could not be laid completely upon the Wensbury clan. The latter, struggling for economic survival on account of all their money having been exchanged for the now valueless currency of the former Confederate States, resented the comparative affluence of their neighbours. Maudlin had had the foresight to retain well over half of his finances in negotiable gold coinage.

A further bone of contention had become a factor to increase hostility. While the terrain for hundreds of square miles around had never known a fence, each family had laid claim to a large area as their respective holdings. Wisely, in the days when they had settled in the vicinity, they had accepted that a strip of land a mile wide on each bank of the easterly flowing Owl Fork of the Lampasas River—which formed the boundary between their ranches—should be considered as a kind of ownerless buffer state common to them both. As each faction's domain was adequately watered from other sources, there had been nothing to be lost through the agreement.

The arrangement had continued to operate in a satisfactory manner, despite the growing antagonism following the War, while there was only a limited market for the enormous numbers of longhorn cattle which flourished across the whole of the Texas range country and offered practically the sole source of income.[3] However, there were now vastly more lu-

3. It would be many years before "black gold," oil, became an important factor in the economy of Texas. Neither cotton or other forms of crop-growing were carried out extensively. "Mustanging," the commercial catching and training of wild horses—as is described in *44 Calibre Man* and *A Horse Called Mogollon*—did not offer large scale employment or revenue.

crative sources of wealth[4] than those at the hide and tallow factories[5] which had formerly presented the major means of selling the livestock. With the animals commanding far higher prices than the four or so dollars a head paid by such establishments, there began to be controversy over the ownership of the unbranded progeny of equally unmarked cattle that occupied the "Fork Range." As the longhorn was notoriously a great traveller, the fact that they could be found to the north or the south of the boundary stream meant nothing.

Soon, a further cause of aggravation had ensued. Rumours had begun to circulate that Maudlin's Leaning M insignia of ownership was being applied to calves whose mothers bore the Circle W brand of the Wensbury ranch and vice versa. None of the accusations had been proved, or disproved, so they had persisted. They had added to the exception taken by the younger Maudlins in particular to various Wensbury suggestions about the reason their family had stayed at home during the War.

One of the most strident of the protestors had been Japhet Maudlin. Youngest and most pampered of three brothers, he was hot headed and inclined to arrogant truculence. Although there had been several fist fights and plenty of verbal disagreements between the two families, it had been he who fired the shot that provided the breaking point beyond which there was little hope of obtaining a peaceable settlement. However, it must be admitted that—on this occasion, at least—he had suffered a considerable amount of harassment from the Wensbury who had fallen to his gun and, as such things were judged west of the Big Muddy, the fight had been fair.

However, the latter fact had not influenced the feelings of the Wensbury family. They had issued threats of reprisals and a state of open warfare had come into existence. Nor had they been content to allow it to stay within the bounds of their respective

4. How these came about and were exploited are told in: *Goodnight's Dream* (American title *The Floating Outfit*), *From Hide and Horn, Set Texas Back on her Feet* and *Trail Boss*.
5. The operation of such an establishment is described in: *The Hide and Tallow Men.*

kin's participation. Within a fortnight, both sides had started to bring in professional gun fighters. Of the two, being considerably the more wealthy, the Maudlins had the advantage where the hiring of such expert assistance was concerned.

Furthermore, as was generally the case, the trouble had spread beyond the members of the opposing families and their hired help. With an eye to the future, or because of kinship ties, the majority of the population in Lampasas and the neighbouring Counties started to favour one side or the other. Doctor Leroy was one of the few who had elected to remain neutral. As the only qualified medical man in the area, also being tough and independent by nature, he had declared that he would continue to supply his services where needed. He refused to take up with either faction.

Up to that late spring day, Leroy's pronouncement had met with no objections from the two families. As his only son would be leaving for New Orleans, to commence studies at the Medical College of the Soniat Memorial-Mercy Hospital at the end of the month, they had decided to relax by spending a day hunting. So far, their efforts at finding any suitable game had come to nothing. However, a visit to the property of a widow at the joining of the Owl Fork with its parent, the Lampasas River, had brought information. They had seen a way in which they could combine their sport with doing a favour for the owner, who—in spite of living on the Maudlins' side of the boundary—was also preserving neutrality.

After riding a couple of miles west along the Owl Fork, Doc and his father had come upon something which they felt might repay investigation. Dismounting and leaving their well trained horses ground hitched by allowing the split ended reins to dangle from the shanks of the bits, they had taken their rifles from the saddleboots.

"What do you make of the sign, Lil Doc?" Leroy inquired, standing with his Henry repeating rifle across the crook of his left arm.

Black haired, slightly over medium in height, but thickset and powerful—Doc inherited his slender physique from the maternal side of the family—Leroy was a good looking man whose always pallid face sported a neatly trimmed black moustache and chin beard. He wore the attire of a working cowhand much of the time, particularly when making house calls beyond the town limits of Lampasas. An excellent rifle shot, he was reasonably competent with the walnut handled Colt 1860 Army revolver that generally hung holstered at his right thigh.

Holding a vertical action Lee single shot cartridge rifle at the wrist of the butt with his right hand and resting its barrel on his shoulder, Doc Leroy looked down. Even in those days, he could have passed as a Texas cowhand as far as his clothing went. An ivory butted Army Colt, won the previous year in a calf roping contest at the Lampasas County Fair, rode in a carefully designed and tied down holster on his right thigh.

Ahead of the two men, the ground showed a disruption similar to that which could have resulted if hogs—wild, feral or domesticated—had been rooting. However, he knew that the former variety of the species *Suidae* did not exist in Texas, nor were the other two abundant in the area. What was more, the few hoof marks that showed were closer in their resemblance to sheep. Except, again, such creatures were not to be found anywhere around Lampasas County. Such scats as had been ejected by the animals' bodily functions were larger and more segmented than the small, single pellets passed from sheep. Finally, a number of cactus plants in the feeding area showed teeth marks from between about eighteen and twenty-four inches above the ground.

"*Javelina*, Sir John," Doc stated, using the corruption of the term "surgeon" which he and his mother always employed when addressing the head of the family. "Likely the same bunch that played hell with the Widow Simcock's truck garden last night."

"They look to be a mite bigger than most peccaries I've come across," Leroy pointed out, applying the alternative name for animals of the *Tayassuidae* family.[6] "In fact, I've never seen such a high average size."

"Or me," Doc conceded, having done a fair amount of

---

6. *Javelina* is the Spanish name, referring to the animal's javelin-like tusks. Peccary derives from a Brazilian Indian word, *peccari*, which means the "animal that makes paths through the woods."

hunting and learned much about such things from the older members of the parties. "Anyway, they're not too far ahead and should be lying up in the shade for the afternoon. How do you want to go after them?"

"I know *you* don't care for *walking*," Leroy answered, with a smile. "But we can move some quieter that way and won't be so likely to spook them."

Returning his father's grin, Doc agreed with the comment. Having been the subject of a fair amount of hunting, most of the surviving wild animals had developed a healthy caution and mistrust where human beings were concerned. Some could even detect the difference between the sounds made by an unburdened horse and one which was carrying a rider.

There was another, more important, consideration behind the decision. A peccary could gallop at around twenty-five miles per hour for a short distance, but was unable to outrun a man on a horse. While Doc and his father could be numbered among those people who enjoyed the light coloured, dry textured flesh of the little pig-like creatures, they were after sport rather than hunting for the pot. So they wanted the pleasure of making a successful stalk and did not particularly care whether they ended it by taking a kill or not. Going on foot would, therefore, be better fun and was more suited to their needs.

As a precaution, knowing that they might be away for about an hour, Doc and his father fastened their horses reins to the branches of a bush. Before moving off to track down their quarry, Doc took a .45 calibre centre-fire cartridge[7] from the box in his jacket's left hand pocket. Normally, he would have been armed with a Henry. A toggle link in the mechanism had broken,[8] so he had left it for repairs with the local gunsmith and was using the single shot Lee. There was a bullet in the rifle's chamber, but he wanted to have a reserve readily available. With

---

7. Centre-fire cartridge: one where the primer to detonate the firing charge is set in the centre of the cartridge case's base. In rim-fire cartridges, as the name suggests, the priming charge was inserted all around the rim of the base. J.T.E.
8. A description of a toggle link breakage and how it could be repaired is given in: *Calamity Spells Trouble*.

that in mind, carrying the Lee in what bayonet fighters described as the "high port" and allowing it to be brought into action rapidly, he held the replacement round with its base gripped between the third and little finger of his right hand.

Before the hunters had gone a quarter of a mile, beyond a rim that they were approaching they could hear the steady, low monotone chatter of short grunts, soft yapping and barks by which the *javelinas* kept in contact with the other members of the sounder among the fairly thick bushes where they were feeding and resting. What was more, as the wind was blowing towards the human beings, it carried the pungent aroma from the large and open musk gland in the centre of each animal's back about eight inches ahead of the tail.

Approaching cautiously, down the more open side of a wide valley in the bottom of which their quarry was located, Doc and his father halted at the first sight of some of the sounder. They knew that the *javelinas*'s eyesight left much to be desired, but both hearing and sense of smell more than made up for the former's deficiencies.

"Whooee, Sir John!" Doc breathed after staring at the animals for a moment. "I've never seen *javelinas* like these before."

Standing about twenty-five inches high, with a length of around forty-five inches, the nearest of the animals had the typical appearance of the *Tayassa* genus. Its sturdy, compact body had such a short, thick neck that it almost seemed non-existent. It had slender legs with sharp pointed hooves and a tiny, thin tail. The head was large and wedge-shaped with small eyes. It tapered sharply forward from the tiny ears to a snout which could only be matched by that of a pig. Unlike a pig's tusks, the upper pair were directed outwards and upwards and those in the lower jaw pointed outwards and backwards, the long canine teeth of its upper jaw pointed down and those in the lower jaw projected upwards.

However, as Doc noticed, the animal was somewhat larger than any he had previously encountered. In addition, it was black as opposed to the usual brownish shade and, instead of the collar of white hairs around the shoulders, had only a white area on the lower side of the head.

"Or me, Lil Doc," Leroy whispered back. "But, although I'll be damned if I know how they've got this far north, I've heard of them. They're Mexican white-lipped peccaries and a whole lot meaner than the Texas collared *javelinas* we get around here."

"Do they *taste* as good?" Doc inquired, in no louder tones.

"I don't know," Leroy admitted and snapped the butt of the Henry to his shoulder in a deftly performed motion.

"Let's find out." Then, throwing aside any attempt to silence, he gave a whoop of "Yeeagh!"

Instantly, the nearest of the peccaries let out a barking, cough-like alarm call and spun around to dash for the nearest cover. Equally startled and alerted to the danger, the others duplicated the warning cry and started to dash away as fast as their apparently puny little legs could carry them.

Satisfied in having achieved their purpose of stalking the peccaries, neither Doc nor his father wanted anything so easy as a shot at the motionless animals. So Leroy had let out the yell to set their quarry into motion. However, part of the fun was in trying to take his son unawares. So he had given no warning of his intentions.

Having hunted with his father many times, Doc had anticipated what would happen. So his own rifle had risen even more quickly than the repeater. He was already squinting along the thirty-two and a half inch round barrel when the Rebel war yell rang out. Wishing that he was carrying his Henry instead of the more cumbersome Lee, he took aim and began to depress the trigger.

Lining his sights on one of the swiftly departing black-bristle covered shapes, Leroy learned that his ploy had not succeeded. Even as his rifle's hammer was liberated and snapped forward, he heard the bark of the Lee from outside his range of vision.

Although Doc kept the barrel swinging—to compensate for the way his target was moving to the recoil kick came, his instincts told him that he had not held as true as he would have wished. Raked across the rump by the bullet, the largest of the fleeing peccaries let out a squeal of pain and increased the pace of its flight. At the same moment, conscious of the crack from the Henry's detonation, much to his chagrin he saw another of the animals suddenly turn a somersault and crash to the ground. Then he heard the clicking as his father operated the lever to put the repeater through its reloading cycle.

Silently cursing the misfortune that had left him equipped in such an unsuitable manner, Doc struck the Lee's hammer with the heel of his right hand. Doing so caused the breech to depress and, as the ejector tossed out the empty cartridge case, exposed the opening of the chamber. On being inserted, the rim of the bullet that had been held between his fingers caught and moved the extractor to its earlier position. Automatically, as the round was fully seated in the chamber, the mechanism's two-piece mainspring went into action. One leaf operated the hammer, thrusting it back to the cocked position and the other closed the breech block ready for firing.

Although the Lee was a comparatively simple weapon to handle, by the time Doc was seating the bullet, his father's Henry spoke again and a second peccary collapsed in its tracks. The rest of the sounder's visible members disappeared into the thicker undergrowth with all the facility offered by having diamond-shaped bodies ideally adapted for rapid movements through such terrain. If the squeals and other sounds were any guide, their concealed companions were also taking an equally rapid departure.

"What's up, Lil Doc?" Leroy inquired, obviously hiding a grin, as he lowered the smoking repeater and looked at his son. "I know that we want to scare them well away from the Widow's truck garden, but I thought you'd at least *try* to down one for us to take to Reverend Gazern."

"That's why I only nicked mine," Doc answered, favouring the Lee with a malevolent scowl. "I've never forgiven him for taking a switch to my hide that time when I was a button and he caught me fishing on the Lampasas one Sunday afternoon."

"That's mean, boy, *real* mean, holding a grudge for so long," Leroy pointed out cheerfully, starting to walk towards the nearer of the peccaries he had shot. "You must get it from your momma's side of the family."

"Now it's strange *you* should reckon that, Sir John," Doc countered, advancing at his father's side. "Momma always lays my ornery streak on you."

For all their conversation, the hunters held their rifles ready for use and kept a constant watch upon the two motionless animals. They knew that, mild as it might be under normal conditions, the Texas collared peccary was capable of inflicting painful and serious injuries with its tusks when roused or cornered. Being larger and even better equipped for offense, the white-lipped visitors from south of the Rio Grande was likely to prove a far more dangerous adversary. However, while neither regretted having done so, the precautions proved needless. Both of the *javelinas* had been killed instantaneously.

"They must have had heart seizures," Doc commented dryly, ignoring the evidence of injury shown by each carcass.

"Those bullet holes in their ribs could have had something to do with causing it, though," Leroy replied.

"Now me," Doc drawled, "not wanting to ruin good eating meat, I was going for a head shot."

"Trust you to try for the easiest part," Leroy sniffed. "These fool critters are nearly two thirds head."

"Nore more than *half*," Doc objected and surveyed the dense undergrowth with some disfavour. Like any true sportsman, he would never leave a wounded animal to suffer a slow and lingering death if it could be avoided. "Well, I suppose I'd best go and take a look for it."

"We'd best trade rifles then," Leroy suggested. "That Lee's a mite cumbersome to take in there and too slow to reload."

"I'll leave it out here," Doc answered. "Happen you'll back me with the Henry, I'd soon count on my old Colt in th—"

At that moment, the sound of rapidly approaching hooves came to the hunters' ears. Looking around, they saw five riders—four of whom were carrying rifles—coming down the side of the valley at a gallop.

Identifying one of the party and guessing who the rest might be, Doc and his father doubted whether they were merely on a hunting trip and coming to discuss the possibility of obtaining some sport.

CHAPTER TEN

Being a Doctor Might Not Save You

"What do you reckon you're doing on *our* land?" demanded the man who Doc Leroy and his father had recognized, as the five riders brought their horses to a halt in a rough half circle.

"*Your* land?" queried Doctor Eldridge Jason Leroy, M.D., studying the speaker coldly, but without ignoring his four companions.

About a year older than Doc, the same height and build, Japhet Maudlin sported the attire of a range-country dandy and carried a Colt 1860 Army revolver with fancy Tiffany grips in a low hanging holster. Brown hair, allowed to grow longer than the general fashion of the West, framed a somewhat weak face set in what he regarded as an expression of truculent arrogance.

Lounging on the well made low horned, double girthed saddle of a fine palomino gelding, Maudlin scowled at the reply. He had never forgotten the occasion, some eight years ago, when he had attempted to bully the pallid and studious-looking new boy at the Lampasas schoolhouse. Much to his discomfiture, he had learned that Doc was well versed in self defense. Although he had come through it unmarked, Leroy had been a noted boxer in his younger days and had taught his son to be competent at bare handed fighting.

Conscious of Maudlin's thinly veiled hostility, Doc and his father were more interested in the other members of the party.

With them at his back and, presumably, under his command, the rancher's youngest son could be a dangerous proposition.

Even at so early an age, Doc had had sufficient contact with real and pretended hard-cases to be able to pick out the genuine from the would be. While all three were hired gun hands, in his opinion only one of them was worthy of notice. The rest were much alike. Dressed somewhat better than working cowhands, except when the latter were visiting town to spend a month's hard earned wages, they were tough faced and their low tied guns gave a clear indication of how they earned their living.

Although not quite as tall and well built as any of his companions, the exception was in every way more impressive; even though he alone did not hold a rifle. His clothing was neat and functional, without being flashy or fussy. It was the kind of attire a well-to-do rancher might wear when riding his own range. One each side of his two and a quarter inch wide black leather waist belt, in a form-fitting Missouri skin-tight type of holster, a fancy Colt Pocket Pistol revolver pointed its ivory handle forward so it would be accessible to either hand. Good looking, his tanned features showed neither the vicious hardness of the hired fighting men, nor the truculent weakness of Maudlin. Instead, for all its lack of expression, there was a suggestion of strength and intelligence mingled with bitterness in its lines.

Even without noticing the initials carved on the matched Colts' ivory grips, Doc and his father could have identified the man. They had heard plenty of talk about him and had had him described more than once, although he had only been in the area for a couple of weeks. His name was Hayden Paul Lindrick. Formerly a promising officer in the Confederate States' Army, he had turned to his present trade on finding his family had been murdered and their home burned by carpet-baggers who were serving in the much hated State Police which had been organized to replace the Texas Rangers after the end of the War Between the States. Fast, deadly, intelligent, he had attained some prominence in his profession and had been brought in by Taylor Maudlin as boss gun.

"It's *our* range!" Japhet Maudlin stated. "And we don't

take kind to *anybody* coming on it for *any* reason, 'less they ask us first."

"Do you know something?" Leroy growled, paying no attention to anybody other than the rancher's son. "I'm pleased I wasn't here when you were born. I'd hate like hell to think I'd brought *you* into the world."

"What do—?" Maudlin began, then anger darkened his face as his far from brilliant intellect deduced the meaning of the comment. Although the rifle across his knees was pointing away from the required direction, he made as if to rectify it, going on, "Why you—!"

"Don't!" Leroy warned, standing with the Henry in a position of far greater readiness, but too wise to move it into alignment. "You'd never get it turned my way. And, if you do get yourself shot, it's a long ride to another doctor and I'll be damned I'll take my own lead out of you."

"Hold it!" Lindrick snapped, his voice commanding and bearing the accent of a well educated Southron. The words caused the other three gun hands to refrain from any movements they might be contemplating and he kept his hands resting on the dinner plate sized horn of his elegant single girthed Mexican saddle as he looked the hunters over from head to foot. "Do you mind if I ask who you are, sir?"

"My name's Leroy," Doc's father introduced, wanting to avoid a confrontation and sensing that the boss gun would be the deciding factor in doing so. "I'm a doctor and this is my son."

"Just because you're the local sawbones—!" Maudlin spat out, but the words trailed off as Lindrick turned a coldly prohibitive gaze upon him and brought an end also to his intention of forcing the issue by turning the rifle.

"It looks as if you've had a successful hunt, Doctor," the boss gun remarked, after he was sure that he had brought the ill-advised actions and words of his employer's son to an end.

"Not as well as we'd like to have had," Leroy contradicted, making a gesture of goodwill by taking his right hand from the Henry and waving towards the nearby bushes. "They raided Widow Simcock's truck garden last night and we figured to

teach them a little more respect for people's property. One
went in there wounded—"

As if wishing to prove the last remark, the big boar peccary
injured by Doc burst out of the bushes. While fleeing, it had
been startled by a cougar that had been sleeping near a kill.
Reversing its direction with the wonderful dexterity of its
kind, the boar had darted back at such a pace that it emerged
from concealment before it realized what had happened. Finding itself confronted by more enemies at a closer proximity
than the cougar had been and already furious with the pain
from the otherwise not too serious graze caused by the bullet,
it was disinclined to attempt further evasion. Instead, letting
out a scream of rage, it launched an attack at the nearest of the
human beings.

The sight of the furious creature hurling their way frightened the horses. With its black bristles erected, the peccary
looked far larger than its sixty-five pounds weight as it
launched itself into the air with Leroy as its objective. Furthermore, as Doc and his father had mentioned, its head was large
in proportion to the rest of the body. So the jaws, when open
to emit a rage-filled squeal, displayed an impressive gape
which caused the wickedly sharp tusks to appear even longer
and deadly than they were. Not that their true size was anything to be regarded lightly. So the vision was sufficiently
menacing to set the five horses displaying their displeasure
and alarm.

An instant after the boar *javelina* had erupted from among
the bushes, pandemonium reigned in front of them.

Caught unawares as his mount reared, Maudlin slid backwards off the cantle of his saddle. With his highly prized
Winchester Model of 1866 rifle—which until recently had
been sold as the "New Improved Henry"—flying from his
hands, he landed rump first on the ground and counted himself
lucky that nothing worse happened. Lashing out with its hind
legs, his gelding went buck jumping away.

One of the lesser hired guns was pitched off by his horse's
wild reaction. Only by dropping their rifles and using both
hands to grab and hold grimly on to the leather were the other
two able to stay on their saddles. They were too engrossed in

doing so to even think of regaining control of the panic-stricken animals.

Of Maudlin's party, Lindrick came off best. A superb rider and unencumbered by holding weapons, as well as being possessed of excellent reflexes, he retained his seat with no difficulty against the somewhat less violent response of his well trained blaze-faced brown gelding. In fact, while bringing the animal back under command, he was able to watch what went on around him.

The boss gun saw something enlightening which he, with his specialized knowledge of the subject, was well equipped to understand.

Appreciating the danger and discovering that he was the target for the reprisals, Leroy brought his right hand back to the wrist of the Henry's butt. At the same time, he essayed a leaping turn which was intended to carry him away from the attacking beast. Instead, his right foot caught against a clump of grass and he tripped. Sitting down involuntarily, he felt his grip on the rifle jarred loose. While he contrived to avoid releasing it, he knew that he could not tighten his hold and put the weapon into use quickly enough to save himself.

Observing his father's dire predicament, Doc was aware of the problems he was facing in the matter of rendering assistance. Although reliable enough, the Lee was far from a handy weapon. Nor was he willing to take a chance upon its single shot capacity with so much at stake. There was, he considered in a flash of rapid thinking, only one suitable solution.

Despite his horse still moving restlessly, although it was calm compared with those of his companions, Lindrick turned his right hand palm out and snapped it around the revolver on the off side of his belt. Using the high cavalry-twist method, he drew and cocked the weapon. Even as he did so, he realized that trying to save the Doctor would be anything but a simple matter. Effectively as he could handle the comparatively small Colt in ordinary combat conditions, he was cognizant with its limitations. It was designed as a fairly easy to conceal close quarters arm. At the distance separating him from the enraged and swiftly rushing *javelina*, particularly while mounted, the best he could hope to achieve was an exceptionally fortunate hit which would turn the animal from its intended victim.

Pivoting towards his quarry, allowing the Lee to drop unheeded, Doc set his weight on spread apart feet and slightly bent legs. Down dipped his right hand, to enfold the ivory grips and lift the streamlined Colt from its contoured holster. Thrusting it out at waist level, he thumbed back the hammer and directed the seven and a half inch long "Civilian pattern" round barrel[1] by the instinct he had acquired from long practice.

In just under a second from the first movement of his right hand, Doc turned loose a shot. His aim proved to be adequate, if not completely successful. The .44 calibre round lead ball hit the peccary in the ribs. Driven by twenty-eight grains of black powder, the charge from an Army Colt could not match the shock power of its illustrious "elder brother," the Colt Dragoon Model of 1848—which would accept *forty* grains, the same amount as would later be handled by the Winchester Model of 1873 *rifle*—it was still far from a puny weapon. Unfortunately, the bullet had struck a little too far back. Although the peccary was knocked from its feet, it was up fast and lunged onwards.

Before Lindrick could align his Pocket Pistol in a satisfactory manner, he heard the deep bark of Doc's Colt. The sound caused him to look in its direction and he could appreciate just how swiftly the youngster must have moved to draw and fire the weapon. What was more, he found himself impressed by the way in which Doc was electing to continue dealing with the situation.

Utilizing the rising thrust of the Colt's recoil, the youngster elevated it to eye-level. While his right hand's thumb was cocking back the hammer, the left's palm joined it to cup under the revolver's butt. Doing so produced a steadier base from which to take aim. He made the most of it. Sighting fast, he squeezed the trigger. This time, the bullet achieved its pur-

1. Colt 1860 Army revolvers intended for purchase by the military had eight inch barrels.

pose by striking just below the peccary's ear. Killed instantly, it collapsed as if it had been boned and landed with the tip of its snout almost touching his father's feet.

"Whooee!" Leroy ejaculated, staring down at the twitching body. Then he raised his gaze to his son and went on, "*Gracias*, Lil Doc."

"*Es nada*, Sir John," the youngster answered, trying to conceal his relief and twirling away the Colt. "Wasn't he an ornery son-of-a-bitch?"

"If he wasn't, he'll do until one comes along," Leroy admitted and stood up.

"God damn it!" Japhet Maudlin's voice raised in a wail. "Get after my son-of-a-bitching hoss, one of you!"

At the anguished-filled words, doc and his father remembered the quintet and turned to find out what had been happening. They found that one of the hired guns had also lost his mount. Along with Maudlin's palomino, it was bolting back in the direction from which it had come. Nor were any of the other three men offering to give chase. Although they had not been thrown, two of the hard-cases were still in difficulties with their restive animals. However, despite being in a position to attend to the request from his employer's son, Lindrick was not offering to do so. Instead, the boss gun was gazing at the hunters and held his right hand revolver.

"That was real good shooting, young feller," Lindrick declared, swivelling the weapon deftly to catch it around the chamber and return it to its holster.

"Thanks," Doc replied, knowing that he was receiving what amounted to an accolade from a top professional. "With daddy here deciding to sit down and take a rest, I figured *somebody* should ought to do *something* and I couldn't think of anything else to do."

"Somebody go catch my blasted hoss, god damn it!" Maudlin almost screeched, rising and rubbing his rump.

"Get on behind Shabber," Lindrick suggested, although the words came out more in the nature of a command. "Czonka, let Waltham ride double with you."

Once again, the boss gun's words received more attention than those of their employer's son. Bringing their mounts back under control, the mounted hard-cases each carried out his instructions. Scowling balefully, Maudlin retrieved his rifle and swung up behind the tall, gaunt Len Shabber. Having regained his feet and weapon, the more blocky, bearded Hank Waltham accepted the stirrup offered by Lazlo Czonka, the burliest of them all.

"What about them two?" Maudlin asked, with what truculence he could muster, once he had settled as comfortably as possible.

"I'll 'tend to them," Lindrick promised. "And the sooner you get after your horse, the quicker you'll be able to get back on it."

Taking what was clearly something much stronger than a hint, Shabber set his mount into motion without reference to the wishes of his employer's son. Nor did Czonka show any great desire to linger. Since they had taken their present employment, before in Shabber's and Waltham's case, all of the trio had learned that Lindrick took his position as their superior *very* seriously and had a forceful way of ensuring his orders—even when made in the form of a suggestion—were carried out.

Waiting until the two double-loaded horses were following the unmounted pair that had already departed, Lindrick rose closer to Doc and his father. There was little expression on the boss gun's face, although a sardonic smile had twisted briefly at his lips as he had looked at Maudlin's back.

"Something tells me you're not impressed by young Japhet Maudlin," Leroy remarked, without bothering to hold the Henry in a position of readiness.

"Do I have to be?" Lindrick countered in a flat tone.

"You work for him," Leroy pointed out.

"I work for his father," Lindrick corrected.

"Huh huh!" Leroy grunted. "Has Taylor Maudlin took it on himself to try and close this part of the 'Fork Range'?"

"Only to the Circle W—and its supporters," the boss gun replied. "It's a precaution against—incidents."

"This's always been open range," Leroy commented, waving his left hand at their surroundings. "Maudlin doesn't have any more right, or title to it than Boone Wensbury has from the other bank of Owl Fork to Slipper Creek."

"Right and title are just words open to definition, Doctor," Lindrick answered, still showing not the slightest emotion. "You've no doubt heard the legend of the Ancient Roman general who, when asked for his authority to carry out an unpopular act, pointed to his assembled Legion and said, 'There it is'?"

"I've heard of it," Leroy admitted, studying the other man and being impressed by what he saw. There, unless his judgment of character was at fault, was no ordinary hired gun fighter with brains only in the trigger finger. Lindrick was intelligent and well educated, a formidable combination for one in his trade. "I've also read Gibbon's *Decline and Fall of the Roman Empire*."

"I have too, Doctor," the boss gun conceded. "But there is another anecdote which covers it. A man was hired to help build a house and found the foreman was a hard driver who never let up. So he complained and said, 'Don't forget, Rome wasn't built in a day.' The foreman replied, 'That's because I wasn't running the job.' "

"I've heard *that* story, too," Leroy said, and could not hold back a smile.

"From what I've heard, Doctor," Lindrick went on, with just a momentary relaxation of his impassive expression. "You've passed the word that you won't take sides in this affair."

"I won't," Leroy confirmed and, at his side, Doc tensed slightly.

"That's a good way to be, as long as you're let do it," Lindrick drawled, his gaze fickering briefly to the youngster and returning to the other man. In the same unemotional tones, he went on, "You probably don't need this advice, but step *very* carefully when you're dealing with hired guns—or young hot-heads—on *either* side. Being a doctor might not save you if one of them gets riled."

"I'll keep it in mind," Leroy promised and meant what he said. "But about Maudlin trying to close—"

"Not *trying*, Doctor, *closing* the 'Fork Range' south of the

Owl Creek," Lindrick interrupted. "But only to the Circle W and its allies."

"And suppose he decides that takes in *everybody* who isn't for him?" Leroy asked.

"In that case, Doctor," Lindrick replied and started to rein his horse around. "I'll do what I'm being paid to do. *Adios*."

"Now *there* goes a man I'd hate to tangle with, Lil Doc," Leroy announced to his son, watching the boss gun riding away.

"He's a strange one," Doc admitted. "I've seen my share of bad *hombres* already, Sir John, but he's way different from any of them."

"That's what makes him so dangerous," Leroy stated, then shrugged. "Come on. We've got work to do before we can take these peccaries back to town."

Oblivious of the comments that were being made about him, Lindrick passed over the top of the slope. Looking ahead, he discovered that his companions were halted about half a mile away. Although they had already recovered the two horses, it had not been by their own efforts. Four more riders were with them. He did not need to go any closer to identify the new arrivals.

There was nothing of his youngest son's dandified appearance about Taylor Maudlin. Tall, heavily built, with a strong, tanned and heavily moustached face, his garments were of no better quality than those of the three men who were with him. Two were cowhands who had been in his employment for a number of years and the last was his eldest son, Frank, looking like a younger version of himself. All of them were well armed, but only the latter carried his Army Colt in a holster that would allow it to be drawn with any speed.

"We heard shooting and came over to find out what was happening, Mr. Lindrick," Taylor Maudlin explained, as his boss gun rode up. Although hard, his voice was that of a man with a good education. "Japhet here says you had a run in with Doc Leroy and his young 'n'."

"Hardly that," Lindrick answered. "They're out hunting—"

"On *our* land!" Japhet protested. "You said we should run everybody off'n it, daddy."

"I said you were to run anybody from the Circle W off," Maudlin corrected.

"Way *I* see it," Czonka put in. "Anybody who ain't for us is again' us."

"I can't recall anybody having asked *you* to make *that* decision," Lindrick commented, looking straight at the speaker.

For a moment, Czonka met the boss gun's cold and challenging eyes. Then, although he was still nursing his Spencer carbine and the other's hands were empty, being aware of his limitations, he dropped his gaze. In spite of his submissive behaviour, a dull red tinge crept to his cheeks and his brows creased in a scowl at the humiliation.

"I don't *like* having to repeat myself," Lindrick said quietly, satisfied that he had re-asserted his superiority over his subordinate and knowing he had aroused the other's enmity, but not greatly perturbed by the thought. "I'll do it *this* time. One of the quickest ways you'll find to bring down the law in an affair of this kind is to start making trouble for people who aren't actively involved."

"Law?" Japhet snorted. "Dirk Damon throwed in his sheriff's badge and there's nobody else wanting to take it up."

"That's true," Lindrick conceded. "But don't sell him short. He didn't quit because he was scared, but because he knows there's right and wrong on both sides."

"Is that how you figure it, Mr. Lindrick?" Frank Maudlin inquired, having learned that the boss gun did not encourage anybody to adopt a first name basis.

"I'm not paid to care whether there is, or isn't," Lindrick answered evenly. "Only to do what I'm hired for. See your father comes out the winner."

"Which you've said all along and *I'm* happy with," Maudlin declared, throwing a frown at his oldest son. "So we'll hear Mr. Lindrick out."

"There's more than the local law to be taken into consideration," the boss gun went on.

"Davis's stinking State Police?" Japhet scoffed, bringing his father's disapproval in his direction.

"Don't sell *them* short, either," Lindrick advised, after the youngest son had been quelled by Maudlin's angry order to 'keep shut'. "I know what a lot of them are like. But Governor Davis is one smart politician. He's seen the money that's been brought in already by trail drives and knows there'll be more coming. Enough to start setting Texas back on her feet fast. Davis knows what *that* could mean. So he's trying to make people forget how the State Police have been acting and show he's trying to bring fair and upright law and order. To do it, he's taken on some mighty smart, tough and capable peace officers."

"Who's worried about them?" Japhet grumbled, then cringed as his father's furious gaze whipped around at him.

"I'm not," Lindrick admitted. "But your father is. He *knows* that his affair has to be settled locally and without drawing too much attention—"

"That doesn't worry me too much," Maudlin objected, but there was a lack of conviction in his voice.

"It's your decision," Lindrick answered. "But you hired me to give you advice on this sort of thing. One thing I've learned is not to let the other have something they can use to turn public sympathy against you. Making fuss for, or letting harm come to a man as popular and important to the district as Doctor Leroy would be the quickest way to do that."

CHAPTER ELEVEN

I'll Do What I Have To

"Was I a suspicious man," Dirk Damon declared, looking from the five cards he had just been dealt to the youngest of the four players in the poker game that was taking place in the dining-room of Doctor Eldridge Jason Leroy's combined office and home, "I'd maybe get to wondering how I have a three of spades I saw on the bottom of the deck when I made the cut."

In spite of the nature of his comment, there was a grin on the rugged, freckled face of the red-haired former sheriff of Lampasas County. Big, burly, clad in range clothing, he was a powerful and commanding figure even when—as at that moment—relaxed and in the company of trusted friends.

"It's not sporting to peek at the bottom card when you cut," Doc Leroy protested, without offering to deny the implication of the peace officer's words. "Is it, Joe?"

"According to Hoyle—" began the man to whom the question had been addressed, guessing waht had happened even though he had failed to detect the move when it had been made.

Bare headed, with his black hair greying at the temples to add to his aura of dignity, Joe Brambile looked and spoke more like a wealthy pre-war Southern plantation owner than a successful professional gambler. His lean and aristocratic features were tanned and sported such a neatly trimmed mous-

tache and goatee beard, they might have been given attention
by a master barber. The set of his grey cutaway jacket, frilly
bosomed white silk shirt and black satin bow tie would have
gladdened a tailor's heart. Nor could any fault be found in his
matching trousers and black boots which were shined almost
to a mirror glossiness. Only a slight bulge on his left side
showed where a Colt Pocket Pistol, similar to those carried by
Hayden Paul Lindrick, hung horizontally, instead of vertically,
in a "directional draw" shoulder holster. He was remarkably
fast and accurate with it.

"As far as I know, Hoyle himself never even heard of
poker, much less wrote about it," Doctor Leroy put in, sus-
pecting that his son had employed one of the techniques
learned from Brambile to form the cause of Damon's comment. Like the gambler and the former sheriff, he had noticed
the way in which Doc had held the deck while dealing, but
nothing else. "I just reckon you're a sore loser, Dirk."

"I'm a sore *winner*," Damon corrected, indicating the
stacks of chips heaped before him. "There's all of *three* dollars here and I sure want to hang on to it, not get skinned by
some juvenile card-shark's looks like butter wouldn't melt in
his mouth."

"Hey, momma," Doc called, showing no offense at the
comment. "Didn't you always tell me to treat guests same as I
do the family?"

"I did," agreed the taller and slimmer of the two women
sitting at the other side of the room watching the play with
considerable amusement.

Brown haired and pallid, Aline Leroy was a maturely beautiful woman. The gingham dress she wore showed off her
slender figure. Like her husband, she had earned the respect
of most people in Lampasas County. When needed she handled the duties of midwife, or assisted in the surgical operations performed by Leroy with an efficiency that matched his
own.

Three uneventful days, at least as far as the town of Lampasas was concerned, had gone by since the peccary hunt.
While the Damons were the Leroy family's closest friends and
frequently exchanged visits in the evenings, the arrival that

afternoon of the other guest had precipitated the poker game which was taking place. Nor had the men waited until after dinner before settling down to it.

Ever since Leroy's skill had saved Joe Brambile's life, following a disagreement with a bad loser in a card game which had resulted in his side being torn open by a knife, the gambler had become a welcome visitor. While he was honest himself, he had of necessity learned the ways and methods of cheats. During the period of his recuperation, stating that the knowledge might come in useful later, he had taught Doc much about both sides of his trade. Learning of Brambile's treatment at the family's hands, other gamblers had continued the youngster's education along those lines when passing through Lampasas.

Always eager to improve his manual dexterity, Doc had spent many hours—especially when the weather was too inclement for outdoor activities—working in front of a mirror to perfect the various gambling tricks he had been shown. How well he had done was proven by the way he had contrived to deal several cards from the deck he had previously marked, without either the move or the signs he had applied being detected by his original tutor. Nor did he have any conscience troubles over having done so. For all the stacks of chips on the table, the stakes were very modest. Furthermore, he had decided to hand over any ill-gotten gains—plus donations from the other players as the price of his silence over having tricked them—to his mother to be donated to Reverend Gazern's collection for a new church.

"There now!" Doc ejaculated, with the air of one who stood completely exonerated. "I've already cheated Sir John once tonight. So it wouldn't be right if I didn't do the same to you two guests."

"He gets it from his *mother's* side of the family," Leroy informed the other men, in a stage whisper which was intended to carry beyond their hearing.

"Shall we go and see if their food's ready for them, Mary?" Aline Leroy inquired, in tones redolent of resignation.

"Do they deserve any?" asked the plump and merry-faced Mrs. Damon, enjoying all that was going on.

"No," Aline admitted. "But things *could* be worse."

"How?" Mrs. Damon wanted to know.

"They might stop playing their silly card game and make a barber's shop quartet," Aline explained, loudly enough to make sure that her words would carry to the table. She rose to her feet. "And, if they do *that*, they'll start singing."

Leaving the men to finish the hand without further interruptions, the two wives went into the kitchen. The meal was in the capable care of Molly Down-Stream, the Leroy's maid. A large, fat and cheerful half Mexican-half *Tenawa*—Down Stream—Comanche woman, she had attached herself to the family after Leroy had found and cared for her following an accident which had caused her to be deserted by her people. She had repaid the kindness by becoming exceptionally competent in her household chores. In addition, she had taught Doc much about the Indians' use of various herbs, roots, leaves and plants to produce various potions for treating illnesses of different kinds.

In spite of the younger's successful manipulations, Brambile won the pot. Before they could continue wtih the game, the maid entered.

"You fellers want food, let me get a table," Molly demanded. "None of you play poker worth a damn anyway."

"You know something," Leroy asked the other men, shoving back his chair. "The Comanche men have better sense than we do. They beat their women."

"Why you think I stop here, live with you white folks?" the maid countered.

Laughing and giving the woman best, the men left the table and gathered in front of the fireplace.

"What's happening up this way nowadays?" Brambile inquired, lighting a cigar after having handed his case around.

"Nothing much," answered Damon, as the question had been directed at him. He knew what aspect of local affairs had provoked it. "Not in town, anyways. I don't know about on the range, though. But, if anything's doing, they're keeping it out there."

"Haven't you been trying to find out?" the gambler asked, being aware of how efficiently the other had always carried out his duties as county sheriff and noticing that the badge of office was no longer pinned to his vest.

"I can't say that I have," Damon replied, looking uncomfortable as he made the admission. A conscientious peace officer, he hated to confess even to such good friends that he was being remiss in the performance of his work. "I've turned in my badge, Joe."

"You'd have a good reason for doing it," Brambile declared.

"I see it that way," Damon stated. "Boone Wensbury and Taylor Maudlin've both stood by me any time I've needed to call on them. But neither will listen to reason. Way I see it, neither of them's all the way in the right, or the wrong. So the best I can do is get killed by one or the other, thinking I'm favouring the oposite side."

"I advised Dirk to do it," Leroy put in. "And to send for the State Police."

"It's what I'd have done myself," Brambile declared. "There's no way a local man can stand in the middle when two bunches of hot heads get to feuding. They'll never think he's playing fair with their side."

"That's why I want Dirk to call in the State Police," Leroy pointed out.

"I'd back you on *that*, Sir John," Brambile drawled. "They'd have the authority to deal with it. And, anyway, let some of them get shot trying to do the work they're paid for. It'll make a change."

"There's some real good men being taken on in the State Police now," Damon protested. "And most who do get sent west where—"

"The pickings aren't so good and the risks are greater," Brambile suggested, before the other could finish by saying, "they will do most good." He raised his right hand in a placatory gesture. "I know, Dirk. No decent peace officer likes to hear it said there are dishonest ones around. And with good cause. It pleases *some* people to think that every man wearing a law badge is tarred with the same brush, but don't count me in their number."

"You have to admit the State Police haven't been what

could be called an efficient outfit so far," Doc pointed out. "It'll be a fair time and need a heap of working at before folks change their minds about them."

"That's the truth," Damon admitted, mollified by the gambler's statement. "Anyways, I might not be sheriff now, but I'm still the town—"

"Listen!" the maid called, cocking her head on one side and looking across the room towards what was the front of the building. "Riders coming!"

Hearing Molly's warning, the men stopped their conversation. As she had claimed, somebody was approaching. However, only the rumbling of fast moving hooves reached their ears and they could not make out how many horses were involved. For all that, the pace at which the animals were being ridden through the darkness suggested the matter bringing them was one of great urgency.

An exchange of glances flashed between the men. Although none of them voiced the subject, the same thought was running through their minds.

Was this the first of the area's trouble to be brought into the town?

"Best take a look and find out," Damon announced, striding towards the door which gave access to the building's entrance hall.

"Four of them, sounds like," Doc remarked, as he, his father and Brambile followed the other guest out of the sitting-room. "They've passed the jailhouse, could be coming this way."

"Could be," Damon agreed, lifting his Confederate States' Cavalry weapon belt—with an Adams Army revolver in its open topped holster—from where he had left it hanging on the hat-stand by the front door.

"It doesn't *have* to be somebody from one of the ranches," Leroy pointed out, as his bulkier guest strapped on the belt.

"Nope, it doesn't," Doc agreed, duplicating Damon's actions with his rig which had also been left on the rack. "Only, like Dirk, I'll feel a whole heap more comfortable dressed until I know for sure."

"The trouble with you, young feller," Brambile remarked,

watching Doc buckle on the belt. "Is that you've got no faith in human nature."

"I do so have," Doc objected, starting to tie the thongs around his right thigh. "It's just people I don't trust. Anyways, I don't see you-all showing good faith by buttoning your jacket."

"The weather's a mite warm for that," the gambler drawled, although—as his audience knew and approved of—his real purpose in keeping his jacket open was to allow unimpeded access to the weapon beneath the garment. "There's no doubt in my mind that they're coming here."

All traces of levity left the men as they listened to the horses drawing to a halt in front of the building and heard the creaking of leather which suggested that the riders were dismounting. Opening the door, Leroy stepped on to the porch and Doc went after him. In spite of having been the first of the party to leave the sitting-room and arm himself, Damon remained with Brambile in the hall. Furthermore, both of them adopted positions which would keep them concealed from the visitors.

One glance was all Doc and his father needed to suggest that their fears might have a firm basis of justification. Two of the riders beyond the picket fence that surrounded the garden were already helping the third from his horse. On the ground by that time, holding a large bandana handkerchief to his brow, Hayden Paul Lindrick was striding swiftly along the path.

"I'd be obliged if you'd close that door before I come any closer, Doctor," the boss gun requested, coming to a stop while still in the darkness and beyond the pool of light from the building. "Under the circumstances, it might not be advisable for my men and I to let ourselves be seen too clearly."

"I'd say that's understandable," Leroy answered dryly, being able to make out sufficient detail to know that the bandana was held in a not entirely successful attempt to staunch a flow of blood from the boss gun's forehead. Then he turned his gaze to where the other two were half carrying and half dragging their companion from the horses. "Go along that path to the right. It will take you to the door of my office and let you stay out of the light."

"*Gracias*," Lindrick replied. "I'll go and take the horses—"

"You'll do as I tell you!" Leroy corrected.

"We haven't been followed, as far as I know," Lindrick began, "but—"

"I don't give a damn whether you have or not," Leroy interrupted. "You've come to me for medical treatment and I'll do what I have to."

"The Circle W might not take kindly to you doing it for us," Lindrick warned. "But you can count on—"

"I'd rather *not!*" Leroy stated definitely, anticipating the other's offer of protection. "I don't work for the Lazy M. Get going, man. You're hurt and it's clear you're not the only one."

"You're right," Lindrick confirmed, glancing behind him as he turned along the junction of the path which led to the right side of the building. "But he's in a worse condition than I am. Get a move on, there."

"Not too damned fast!" Leroy snapped, as the two men began to increase their pace and brought a groan from the third. "God only knows how much damage he's suffered so far, but don't make it even a little bit worse now he's this close."

"Go help your daddy, boy," Damon suggested, *sotto voce* and without revealing himself, after Leroy had led the newcomers away. "Joe and I'll keep an eye on things from in here."

"*Gracias*," the youngster replied, stepping from the porch.

Having been a doctor's wife and lived in the West for many years, Aline Leroy was aware of what such a visit probably portended. So she had already brought a lamp into the office and was lighting a second when her husband arrived.

"I've told Molly to start boiling water, Eldridge," Aline remarked, looking at the men who were following the doctor in to the office. She only employed the family's nickname when they were alone or with very good friends. "Is there anything I can do?"

"Have some coffee ready and bring in a bottle of whiskey," Leroy instructed and turned his attention to the callers.

As the doctor had deduced, Lindrick was injured. Blood smeared his face and his eyes were squinting with the pain he was trying to hide. However, despite the gory mess on his features, Leroy decided that he was the less serious of the two patients.

The men with Lindrick were not hired guns. Instead, they were two of the Lazy M's cowhands. One, in fact, was a good friend of Doc's; a wide shouldered and generally cheery youngster whose mop of reddish brown hair had earned him the nickname "Rusty". Supported between the pair, having been shot in the right side and now almost unconscious, was Taylor Maudlin's second son, Arnold.

"We was riding the herd on—" Rusty Willis began, as Doc followed them in and closed the door.

"I don't give a damn what you were doing and less about what happened!" Leroy snapped. "Set him down as gently as you can on the couch, then get the hell from under my dainty lil feet."

"Yes, sir," assented Rusty obeying with alacrity. He was aware of the doctor's reputation for irascibility when working.

"You go on over and sit at the table, Mr. Lindrick," Leroy suggested. "Let my boy take a look at your head."

"You can let ole Doc there do it safe enough, Mr. Lindrick," Rusty supplemented. "He's's good's his daddy—near on."

"Why thank you 'most to death, *Mr*. Willis, that's real kind of you to say so and I'm sure you've put Mr. Lindrick's mind at rest," Leroy growled, eyeing the young cowhand sardonically. However, he was secretly pleased with the compliment that had been paid, in all sincerity, to his son. "Now, unless you want him to show everybody how good he is at pulling *my* boot out of *your* butt end, watch what you're doing." His gaze swung to Doc and he went on, "And you can stop that grinning, boy. You've a patient waiting for you. Go and do some work."

CHAPTER TWELVE

I Don't Aim To Have It Spoiled

Although Doc Leroy did not lose the grin that had been caused by the interplay between his father and the youngster who was to become an even closer friend in the not too distant future, he turned to carry out the order. Watching the two cowhands lowering their burden gently on to the couch, he walked over to his own patient. Hayden Paul Lindrick went and sat at the table. Trying to remove the bandana, he found that the blood had congealed and was causing it to stick to his brow.

"You don't have to prove to *me* how tough you are," Doc warned, seeing the boss gun wince and then tighten his hold as if meaning to tug the covering free. "Especially if the way you're figuring on doing it's going to make more work for me."

"You're the doctor," Lindrick answered, managing a weak smile as he noticed that the youngster had adopted a similar attitude and tone to that of Doctor Eldridge Jason Leroy, M.D.

"Not yet, but I hope to be," Doc corrected and raised his voice. "Is there any chance of me getting some hot water in here, please?"

"Hot damn if you're not starting to sound like your '*ap*,'" Molly Down-Stream complained, using the Comanche word for "father," as she entered carrying a bowl of hot water and a stack of clean white cloths on a tray. "*One* like him plenty bad enough."

122

"See what a pleasure it is when you hire loyal and respectful help?" Doc inquired, giving his attention to Lindrick. Then
he looked to where his mother was coming in with a bottle of
whiskey and a glass. "We can use that over here, momma.
You're going to need a drink, sir."

"Am I?" the boss gun asked.

"Maybe not while I'm working on you," Doc drawled
cheerfully. "But you sure as hell will when you get the bill for
me doing it."

"In that case, I'd better take one," Lindrick declared, accepting the glass of whiskey Aline Leroy brought over to him.
"My thanks, ma'am."

"Wait until you've tasted it before you thank me," the
woman replied. "It's some Joe Harrigan at the saloon gave my
husband instead of a cash fee. Can I do anything for you,
son?"

"I reckon daddy's going to need you a heap more than I
do," Doc decided, after a quick glance at his father. "Molly
and I can 'tend to things here."

"My thanks, ma'am," Lindrick said, returning the empty
glass. As Aline put it and the bottle on the table, he went on,
"I'm in your hands—doctor."

Asking Molly to fetch him a needle and some of the gut he
might need for sutures, Doc took and soaked one of the pieces
of cloth. Carefully, so as to cause as little pain as possible, he
began to wet the bandana. As the water took effect on the
congealed blood, it came loose and he was able to remove it.

"Whooee!" the youngster breathed, gazing at the vicious
looking furrow in the shape of a flattened "W" that had been
carved across the man's brow. "Mister, I don't know what
you've been hit with, but I'll tell you that you've sure as hell
been hit good."

"I thought I might have been," Lindrick admitted. "Can
you do anything about it?"

"Likely. It's going to need stitching and, even then, you'll
have a scar that'll stay with you for the rest of your days,"
Doc answered and watched the boss gun's eyes flickering to
where his mother and father were already starting to work on
Arnold Maudlin. "You can wait for daddy to get through, only

it could be a fair spell before he's done. Or you can let me do it."

"I'd say let Doc do it, was I you, Mr. Lindrick," Rusty Willis put in. Having been told bluntly by Leroy to go somewhere else he and his companion had returned to the table. "He stitched up a cut I got on my leg three years back and it hasn't's much as dropped off yet."

"With such a recommendation, what have I to lose?" Lindrick said dryly. "Go ahead, *doctor*, but I'd like another drink of that whiskey first."

In spite of his comment, the boss gun knew he had cause to respect Rusty's opinion. Not only did the youngster know something of Doc Leroy's abilities, but he had behaved with courage and initiative in Lindrick's company already that evening.

While accompanying Arnold Maudlin and the two cowhands when they went to relieve the men in charge of a herd of cattle that had been gathered, they had been ambushed. Taking cover behind the trunk of a white oak, Lindrick had told the cowhands to remove Maudlin—who had been wounded in the opening volley—while he held the attackers' attention. Struck on the forehead with a splinter of wood torn from the tree by the impulsion of a rifle bullet and partially blinded as blood cascaded into his eyes, he had been in serious trouble. However, having heard his cry of pain, Rusty had returned. Firing fast as he could work the lever of a borrowed Henry rifle, the youngster had routed their assailants and forced them to withdraw. As they had been closer to town than the ranch house, considering how badly Maudlin was wounded, Lindrick had ordered that they came in to obtain qualified medical attention.

"You want this?" Molly Down-Stream inquired, having collected the items requested and, setting down the tray they were on, indicating an open pill box holding a dark powder. "You didn't say, but I fetched it."

"What is it?" Lindrick asked, putting down the empty glass.

"*Pulvis Hamamelis Virginiana*," Doc growled and, although he did not say, "If you *must* know," the words were implied by his tone.

"Which means the powdered leaves of a witch hazel tree," Lindrick translated. "But I thought—"

"Look, *mister*," Doc interrupted coldly. "Either *you* trust *me* to 'tend to you, or you don't. But, happen its 'yes,' leave me do what I figure needs doing."

"You want for me to whomp him, maybe, Lil Doc?" Molly suggested hopefully, folding her right hand into a fist not much smaller than a ham. "Make him sleep, 'stead of bothering you with fool talk."

"What do *you* reckon, Mr. Lindrick?" the youngster asked threading a needle.

"She may not be respectful, but she's loyal," the boss gun answered. "And I can take a hint. Do whatever *you* decide is necessary, *doctor*."

Accepting the invitation, Doc set about the task. He worked with care and as quickly as possible knowing that the closing of the wound and securing the ligatures could only be accomplished at the cost of considerable pain to the patient. Through it all, although his hands clenched and he occasionally dragged in an extra deep breath, Lindrick made no protest.

While Doc was carrying out the suturing, Molly Down-Stream left the room to have coffee made. She had not returned by the time the youngster had completed the task. Hearing the door open, he assumed it was her returning.

"There're riders coming!" Dirk Damon announced, entering the office. "Sounds to be a fair bunch of them."

"They can't be *our* men this quickly!" Lindrick decided, setting down the glass in which Doc had poured a stiff shot of the whiskey. The lack of colour and haggard expression of his face was mute testimony to the extent of his ordeal. However, in spite of his hands shaking, he looked at the cowhands and began to push back his chair. "We—"

"Stay put!" Doc ordered and the ivory handled Army Colt, which he had not removed while performing the suturing of the wound, leapt from its holster with its hammer clicking back under his thumb. "You're in no damned shape to do anything lively. On top of which, that's as good a chore as I've ever done and I don't aim to have it spoiled by you-all jumping around and busting all my dainty little stitches."

"You Lazy M boys'd best just stand there nice and easy," Damon advised, emphasizing that it was not merely a request by making a gesture with the Adams Army revolver which he had drawn outside the room and held behind his back when coming to deliver his tidings.

"If they're from the Circle W—" Lindrick began, but he had ceased his movements and was sitting still.

"They'll not do *anything* at all in Lampasas," Damon stated. "I only gave up being county sheriff. So I'm still sworn in as town marshal and I'll be damned from here to Sunday and back if I'll have you bringing your troubles into my bailiwick. Which being so, I'll start by taking you three's guns."

"A good leader, which I figure you to be, always shows his men the way, Mr. Lindrick," Doc supplemented, knowing wherein lay the greatest danger and keeping his Colt aligned rock-steady at the boss gun's face. "You do it first."

Providing that not the slightest mistake was made, the easiest person from whom to extract obedience at the point of a gun was an expert in using firearms. Being all too aware of the weapon's deadly potential, he was too wise to take foolish or reckless chances. That particularly applied, as in the present case, when the man being threatened knew he was up against somebody who possessed considerable skill.

Every instinct in Lindrick's body warned him that—young though the other might be—Doc could not be tricked, or bluffed, so as to allow the tables to be turned. There was quiet determination, with neither arrogance, hostility, nor hesitation, about the pallid-faced youngster. He might not care to do it, but he would take whatever steps necessary to enforce his will.

Against that knowledge, Lindrick had his own reputation to consider. There was some pride in his reluctance to obey, but mainly it was caused by the realization of how yielding up his weapons would be construed by his contemporaries. He earned top wages by his skill and by the way in which he could command obedience from lesser hired guns. Once such men heard that he had handed over his weapons, his authority would be weakened and re-establishing it would require that he proved he had not lost his prowess.

"Give them to me, Mr. Lindrick," Aline Leroy suggested, having watched what was happening and guessing at the man's dilemma. Crossing the room, she went on, "If you need them, I'll let you have them back immediately."

"Aren't you needed to help your husband, ma'am?" the boss gun asked, throwing a look of gratitude at the woman and willing to accept any offer which would save him a loss of face, but also knowing how seriously his employer's son was injured.

"I am," Aline confirmed.

"Then I'll not keep you away from your work," Lindrick declared, extracting the Colt Pocket Pistols using only the thumb and forefinger. He pushed them along the table to just beyond his reach. "They'll stay there unless they're needed."

"That's fine," Aline assented and swung her gaze to the two cowhands. "Now it's *your* turn. Would you like to be first, *Regi—Rusty* Willis?"

"I reckon I would at that, Mrs. Leroy, ma'am," Rusty affirmed, being aware that the narrowly averted mention of his hated Christian name 'Reginald' had been anything but accidental. Taking the old Dance Bros. Army revolver from its contoured holster, he walked towards the table, saying, "Come on, Daybreak, do like the lady says."

"Whatever you say, Rusty," replied the second cowhand who, although a few years older, had great respect for his companion.

Although Doc was pleased with the satisfactory way in which the disarming of the trio had been carried out, he wondered how long he could count upon them remaining passive once he had left the office. Yet he believed that the need for him to go might arise. Normally his father could have taken care of the situation, but he was too fully occupied with Maudlin's wound at that moment to be able to do so.

The problem was taken out of the youngster's hands in an unexpected fashion.

"Gambling-man Joe says them fellers get here soon," Molly Down-Stream remarked, ambling into the office with a cocked twin barrelled ten gauge shotgun that seemed almost tiny in her massive right fist. "Wants you and Lil Doc go see what you think about 'em, sheriff."

"We'll do just that," Damon promised. "Where's my wife?"

"Got another shotgun and's in the kitchen, watching back," Molly answered. "Make sure nobody comes fooling around back there."

"*Bueno*!" Damon ejaculated, having shared Doc's concern over the possibility of having to leave Lindrick without adequate supervision and knowing his wife could be counted upon to guard the rear of the building. "Let's go and keep Joe from getting lonely, Doc."

"Reckon I come sit here, out of folks's way," Molly announced, crossing to park her more than ample rump on the table between the boss gun and his revolvers, nursing her own weapon with its barrels pointing his way. "Hey, you Rusty-feller, go into kitchen, find berry pie and bring it back. Only not forget, I know all the other food's is in there."

"I'll fetch it, Molly-gal," the young cowhand agreed delightedly, the maid's berry pies having acquired a local reputation for their succulence.

Deciding that there was little further cause for alarm or concern, Doc joined Damon at the door. Giving a quick glance around and nodding in satisfaction, the peace officer went into the entrance hall. Following, Doc found that the gambler was still standing so he could not be seen from the outside. He had also taken another precaution while they had been otherwise engaged.

"I took the liberty of borrowing this, boy," Brambile announced, gesturing with the Henry rifle that had been hanging over the fireplace in the sitting-room. "Molly let me have some bullets for it."

"One's no good without the other, I'd say," Doc replied. "How do you want us to play it, Dirk?"

"You and I'll go out and see what's doing, then decide which way to head her," the marshal answered, returning his

Adams to its holster. "Might be best at first to have our hands empty."

"You're the dealer," Doc drawled and twirled away the Colt. "Sounds like they're here and aren't waiting to be invited to rest their saddles."

"Sounds like," Damon agreed, drawing similar conclusions from the noises outside. "Can you stay out of sight until you're needed, Joe?"

"Anybody would think you're ashamed to be seen in my company," Brambile answered, although he approved of the suggestion. Glancing cautiously from the window, he became serious. "There are only five of them, but they've come loaded for bear."

Moving across to the gambler's side, so that they could look out equally surreptitiously, Doc and the peace officer gazed across the garden. Having dismounted, the newcomers were examining the horses belonging to the earlier arrivals. Then they came through the gate and walked along the path. In spite of the darkness, they were soon close enough to be identified.

"It's Ted and Lonny Wensbury," Doc announced, having been friendly with the two young men since their schooldays. "And, unless I'm mistaken, that's One-Card Jones with them. But I don't know the other two."

"They're a couple of guns Boone Wensbury's hired," Damon supplied, taking the town marshal's badge from his jacket's pocket and pinning it to his vest. "I saw them when they came through town. They'll be the ones to watch."

"Why sure," Doc agreed, knowing that—as was the case with the two Lazy M hands—the other three were not trained gun fighters, or expert in the use of firearms. "And the ones who'll have the best idea of what chances they can't take."

That last point, as the trio in the hall appreciated, could make the local youngsters more dangerous than the professionals.

"We'd better step out and see what they want," Damon decided.

"I *know* what they want," Doc stated. "It'll be stopping them trying to get it that could give us the trouble."

"It could," the peace officer agreed, stepping towards the door. "Let's go on out and be diplomatic."

"In that case, I'd best go first," Doc suggested. "I've horsed around with Lonny, Ted and One-Card plenty in the past. Could be they'll be inclined to listen to me."

"Go to it," Damon authorized.

"Howdy, Ted, Lonny, One-Card," Doc greeted, walking from the house. At his first word, the quintet came to a halt. Unlike Lindrick on his arrival, they had not stopped clear of the light from the door. All of them made as if to raise their rifles. "Hey, easy there!"

"It's you-all, Doc," greeted Ted Wensbury, the taller and elder of the brothers, relaxing slightly. "It's all right, Talbot, Lington, we know him."

"Looks like you've got some callers, Doc," Lonny went on, jerking his head in the direction of the tethered horses and starting to resume his advance. "We'll just—"

"Keep quiet and stay back," Doc finished for the youngster. "Daddy's working on a bad hurt man—"

"Air that so?" jeered the shorter of the hired guns, also taking a step forward. "Well, seeing's we know how come he got his-self hurt, we'll—"

"That's close enough and too noisy!" Damon warned, stepping across the threshold with his hands behind his back and his holster empty. His appearance brought an immediate end to the resumed advance. "Are you saying's how you *know* what happened to that man who was brought in shot?"

"I can't see's how it comes to being any of your business," the hired gun answered truculently. "But, seeing's how it was us's done it, we should—"

"That being the case," Damon said, almost gently and still without bringing his hands into view. "You're under arrest."

"We're *what*?" the hired gun growled.

"Under arrest," Damon repeated. "You might not know it, but shooting people's against the law and I'm a duly appointed and sworn peace officer."

Listening to the marshal, Doc formed the opinion that he was well pleased with the opportunity he had been presented with by the hired gun's boastfully incautious words. Nor did the youngster need to ask why. They were offering a means by which the quintet could be prevented from causing further trouble that night and, more important, doing it in a way that would remove all suggestion of partiality towards the Maudlins' faction.

"I thought you quit as sheriff!" Lonny Wensbury protested, bristling with what he regarded as righteous indignation.

"I'm still town marshal though," Damon pointed out. "Which makes it my sworn and legal duty to hold you until the county authorities can investigate what you said."

"Like hell you'll hold u—!" began the shorter of the hired guns, making a move at turning his rifle forward.

Steel rasped on leather as the Army Colt flashed into Doc's right hand, lining and cocking all in a single blurring motion. Almost as quickly, Damon brought his Adams-filled fist into view and alignment. Stepping on to the porch, Brambile slanted the Henry towards the quintet in a gesture which left no doubt as to his intentions.

"Drop the rifles!" the peace officer commanded. "*Pronto*, or I'll be taking you for resisting arrest."

"Do it, damn you!" snarled the taller and elder of the hired guns, directing a furious scowl at his fellow tradesman as he complied by allowing his rifle to fall to the ground at his feet. "You stupid son-of-a-bitch, Lington—"

"You must know him *real* well to use his given name," Damon remarked dryly, as the other four discarded their shoulder arms. "Now we'll take the gunbelts and everything'll be more comfortable."

"Our daddy's not going to like this!" Ted Wensbury threatened, unbuckling his gunbelt and tossing it down. "And don't you forget's how *he* voted for you at every election."

"So did most folks, seeing's I was the only candidate," Damon countered, avoiding the error of pointing out that he had received a similar support from Taylor Maudlin. His voice hardened and he continued, "I'm including *you* with the others, Mr. Lington."

"Don't make things any worse than you have already!" the elder hired gun, Talbot, spat at his companion. "Get that belt shed, or I'll do it for you."

"That's fine," Damon said cheerfully, when the disarmament had been completed. "Now I'll take you gents along to the jail and we'll see what the county law thinks about your story. Happen they're satisfied that it was all a mistake, I wouldn't be at all surprised if you wasn't all released without a stain on your characters."

"What about them Lazy M bunch in there?" Ted Wensbury demanded.

"What about them?" Damon countered.

"Are you arresting them?" Wensbury enlarged.

"Not unless *they* start to claiming that they've shot somebody," Damon replied. "As soon as they've had their hurts tended, they'll be going home. By morning, when I allow your case'll have been settled one way or the other, I reckon they'll just be getting there. So there's no reason why you-all should come across each other—happen you show good sense and don't go looking for it to happen."

CHAPTER THIRTEEN

Going There Could Be Dangerous

"Well now, young feller," said the barrel-shaped, jovial-faced Joe Harrigan, who combined ownership of the Pole-Axe Saloon with being a very active mayor of Lampasas. "So you'll be off on Saturday's stage to be made a doctor."

"I'm going to learn how to be one, sir," Doc Leroy corrected.

"Devil's the bit of learning you'll need, me bucko," Harrigan boomed. "Sure and your father's taught you as much's many who've got the blessed letters M.D. behind their names'll ever know."

"*Gracias*, sir," Doc grinned, pleased by the compliment, hoping that he could justify it when the time came. "Excuse me, please. I've got to deliver my present to Josey, or she'll be likely to whomp me for not showing proper respect."

"She's getting a mite too old for games like that, mores the pity; although there might be some who'd say it's high time," Harrigan stated, also grinning, as he looked to where his eighteen year old daughter was greeting some of the other guests. Then the cheerfulness faded and he went on, "Somehow it doesn't seem right for her to be having a birthday party without any of the Maudlins and Wensburys to help celebrate it."

"It doesn't, sir," Doc agreed, remembering the previous years' parties and the fun everybody had had. "But, under the circumstances, it's probably better that they don't come together in town right now."

"That it is," Harrigan conceded with feeling. "Mind you, there's some around who weren't happy with the way you and Dirk Damon handled the Wensbury boys, but it proved to have been right in the end."

"It did," Doc agreed. "At least, as far as the town's concerned. But nothing's changed between the Wensburys and the Maudlins on the range."

Twelve days had elapsed since the members of the two factions had paid their respective visits to the home of Doctor Eldridge Jason Leroy, M.D.

On learning of the measures taken to deal with the Wensburys' party, Hayden Paul Lindrick had conceded that, providing the hired gun, Lington, rescinded the confession, holding the quintet in custody would not be feasible; nor desirable where the welfare of the town was concerned. However, he had promised that he would not attempt to take reprisals for the ambush as long as his former assailants were prevented from trying to repeat the attack. On being given such a guarantee, although clearly suffering from his injury, he had stated that he and the two cowhands would go back to the Lazy M. Allowing them four hours' start, Damon had pretended to accept that Lingford was only displaying a misplaced sense of humour when he claimed to have done the shooting. The men were then released. He had also warned them that they would be advised to return to the Circle W by a route which would keep them well clear of the other ranch, and the older of the hired guns had promised they would do so.

It had been too much to hope that the arrivals of the two parties would have gone unnoticed. However, having the typical Westerners' instinct for the possibility of danger, such of the citizens of Lampasas who were present had kept indoors while awaiting developments. Not until it had become obvious that there was to be no gun play had anybody offered to come and investigate.

On learning what had been done, some of the more timid

citizens and those who tended to favour one side or the other had expressed concern over the wisdom of the marshal's actions. Fortunately, Harrigan and a few other sturdy souls—who had been absent on a coon hunting expedition along the Lampasas River, in which Leroy and Damon would also have been participating if their wives had not made other arrangements—had been summoned from their sport. On their return, they had announced their intention of supporting the peace officer in his efforts to maintain the town's neutrality. Furthermore, they had insisted that Damon should deputize them. By doing so, he would have solid backing when the inevitable protests were delivered from the leaders of the rival factions.

Taylor Maudlin had been the first to put in an appearance. Thinking of the incident, particularly in later years and with the light of greater experience, Doc considered that the way in which the rancher had prepared for his arrival was significant. It was clear that he was determined to avoid any suggestion of bringing trouble in to the town.

Sending Rusty Willis with the information, Maudlin had stated that he would come accompanied only by his wife and sister and that their sole purpose was to collect his wounded son. In addition, he had requested that somebody who was neutral or supported the Wensburys should ride out and verify that he was speaking the truth. Appreciating the wisdom of the suggestion, Harrigan had volunteered.

On reaching the town, despite expressing his gratitude for what had been done on Arnold's behalf, Maudlin had been adamant in the decision to take him back to the Lazy M. Nor, in spite of Leroy's warning that such a course would be highly ill-advised, would he change his mind. He had claimed that the risk of leaving his son in Lampasas was too great. Rather than expose the citizens to the danger of the Wensburys coming to finish the work they had started, he would take Arnold home. Knowing how stubborn the rancher could be, Leroy had warned him that he would accept no further responsibility for the young man's well-being if the removal was performed. When this had produced no change of mind, he had insisted that Arnold was carried in the Rocker ambulance[1] he had purchased for transporting patients.

As a precaution against hostile action on the part of the Wensburys, the vehicle was driven by Doc with Harrigan as an escort until a place, some three miles from the edge of town was reached, where a strong and well-armed party from the Lazy M were waiting to give protection for the rest of the journey. It was clear that Japhet Maudlin and the three hired guns, who had been present, were still resentful over the humiliation they had suffered on the day of the peccary hunt. However, they had done no more than scowl their hostility at Doc.

Before parting company with the rancher, Harrigan warned that he and the other citizens would not countenance the feud being brought into town to endanger their lives and property. Showing a remarkable willingness to oblige, Maudlin had stated that—providing Wensbury would respect the arrangement—he would only allow his men to visit the town on certain designated days and would guarantee their good behaviour.

From what had happened later, it was obvious that Boone Wensbury had been told by one of his supporters what had taken place. Drawing the correct conclusions, he had taken equal care to show that he wished to avoid the stigma of having brought trouble to Lampasas.

Late in the afternoon, Wensbury had sent word that he would like to visit the marshal. He promised that he would bring in the quintet who had been arrested and that they would not be armed. When he arrived, it was found that he had kept his word. However, his party had been accompanied by a lawyer from San Saba who, he said, was representing his family's interests.

According to the five's story, which enlarged what they had said the previous evening, they had been hunting for strays when they were fired upon. So they had shot back, without as far as they knew hitting anybody. After their assailants had fled, they had ridden into town to report the matter to the

1. A description of a Rocker ambulance is given in: *Hound Dog Man*.

authorities. Seeing the horses outside the doctor's house, they had wondered if some more of the Circle W hands had also been under attack. On learning to whom the animals belonged, they had decided to investigate. However, Lingford's statement that he had shot somebody was nothing more than a thoughtless joke for which he was now heartily sorry.

Avoiding any comment upon how he regarded the story, Damon stated that he did not intend to press the matter further unless asked to do so by the Maudlin family. He also delivered a similar warning, with Harrigan's backing, regarding the town's determination to have no part in the disagreement between the two ranches. Displaying an equal desire to appear co-operative, Wensbury had declared that his men would not come into Lampasas on the days allocated to the Lazy M as long as the agreement was respected by the Maudlins.

Much to the relief of everybody in Lampasas, the arrangement had worked so far. Clearly both ranchers had given stringent orders to their respective crews. Each outfit had adhered strictly to the schedules laid down for their visits and the men had been on their best behaviour while in town.

There had only been one incident of note. On the day that the Lazy M had returned the Rocker ambulance, Waltham had started to make drunken threats about taking revenge on the Leroys for almost having caused him to lose his horse. Although Lindrick had come in to have his wound examined and was present at the saloon, it had fallen—surprisingly enough —upon Japhet Maudlin to intervene. Stating that such an idea would not be tolerated by either his father or himself, according to the witnesses who were there, he had ordered the hired gun to forget any such notions.

Although the boss gun's injury was responding in a satisfactory manner and the stitches had already been taken out, the same could not be said for Arnold Maudlin. As Leroy had warned, his father's insistence on moving him—even in such a relatively comfortable vehicle as the Rocker ambulance— had been anything but beneficial to his welfare. In fact, his condition had grown increasingly more critical.

Despite the threat to wash his hands of the matter, Leroy had not deserted his patient. Instead, he visited the ranch and did all he could. At first, he had been far from sanguine over the chances of Arnold's recovery. However, two days ago, the young man had appeared to be rallying. So, having other people requiring his professional attention, the doctor had returned to Lampasas. There had been no news from the Lazy M, so he had assumed that all was going well.

With Doc's departure for medical college imminent and such an important social function as Josephine Harrigan's birthday party that evening, Leroy had decided against making a visit to the Maudlins' ranch that day. He was confident that, if there was any deterioration in Arnold's condition, he would be informed. So he, his wife and son were all set for an evening's relaxation in the company of their friends.

Catching his mother's accusing glance, Doc excused himself from Harrigan and went to deliver his present to the saloonkeeper's pretty daughter. Josey informed him that the half a dozen guests of their own age had planned a surprise for him. Instead of staying at the saloon with the older folks, they were going off on a hay-ride and picnic with him as the guest of honour. Feeling sure that such an affair would be lively and enjoyable, he did not hesitate over accepting the invitation.

Two hours seemed to fly by after the departure of the younger guests. The bar room of the saloon, normally regarded as *terra incognita* where the "good" ladies of the town were concerned, was the scene of more genteel festivities than usually took place there. For all that, everybody appeared to be having a good time. By common consent, the subject of the feud between the two ranches was not mentioned. It looked as though, out of respect for the host and the strength of public opinion, the supporters of the Maudlins and the Wensburys were staying away from the town. There was plenty of good food, a liberal amount of drinks for the male guests and dancing to the music provided by the establishment's small band.

The clock on the saloon's wall was just striking ten when the batwing doors were thrown open. At the sight of the person who was entering, silence dropped over the room. Even the band trailed to a discordant halt.

There was good cause for the reaction. The newcomer was Lonny Wensbury and one glance at him was sufficient to warn everybody present that something was radically wrong. Bare-headed, dishevelled, he had obviously been riding hard. Horror and distress creased his face as he paused, staring around.

"Do-Doctor Leroy!" the youngster gasped, staggering forward.

"What's wrong, boy?" Leroy demanded, leaping forward to help the newcomer into a chair. "Bring him a drink, somebody!"

"Th-There's all hell been let loose along Owl Creek!" Lonny gasped, taking and emptying the glass of whiskey that Harrigan had brought. He glared around wildly and a shudder ran through him as he went on, "All hell—!"

"Take it easy, boy!" Leroy advised soothingly. "Have another drink and tell us what's happened."

"I-It's p-paw!" Lonny groaned, before he could be given another drink. "H-He's dead 'n' T-Ted's bad hit out a-at the Widow Simcock's b-barn. H-He's like t-to die happen he's not get help fast."

Noticing that, although the atmosphere had been growing increasingly more congenial, the youngster's arrival had once again caused the guests to form into three distinct groups—neutral, pro-Maudlin and pro-Wensbury—Leroy had listened to the somewhat disjointed explanation. Before it was half over, the doctor realized that the situation was very grave.

Basically, the story was that one of the Wensbury family had been shot shortly before noon while patrolling along the bank of the Owl Creek. On learning the news, Boone Wensbury had assembled his men and gone in search of revenge. A pitched battle had taken place, going on throughout the whole of the afternoon and into the evening. During the later stages, the rancher had been killed and his son, Ted, seriously wounded. Having rescued his brother, Lonny had realized that he could not hope to take Ted either home or to Lampasas in search of medical assistance. So, reaching the Widow Simcock's property and finding it deserted—she was attending the party—he had left his brother in the barn and come for help.

Hearing the story, Leroy appreciated two significant points. Firstly, despite the death of the Wensbury faction's leader, it seemed as though the fighting on the range would continue. Secondly—and more important to the well-being of Lampasas town—there was now a grave danger that, in spite of all the precautions which had been taken, it might spread to the streets and endanger the population. That was emphasized by the hostility suddenly evident between the supporters of the two factions who were present in the saloon.

"I'm going out there with the Rocker to fetch Ted in!" Leroy stated, accepting that he had no other choice, no matter what the circumstances might be.

"That's what I figured," Dirk Damon answered. "But going there could be dangerous. I'm coming with you."

Grateful as Leroy might be for the offer, he knew he could not accept it. Doing so would leave Lampasas with only Harrigan as a legally appointed law enforcement officer. All the others had only been appointed temporarily and, if it came to a technical point, unofficially. No matter which side of the feud the affected citizens of the town might favour, they were all motivated by family ties, or politics rather than the mercenary reasons of the hired guns. Such men would be more likely to remain passive in the presence of a peace officer they had helped to elect and who had displayed complete impartiality up to that point.

"It isn't that easy, Dirk," the doctor pointed out quietly, but conscious that everybody else was listening to his words. "If *you*, or any of your deputies come, the thing we've all been working to prevent could erupt. Anyways, neither side will make any fuss for me. They all know that I'm completely neutral and they've gone out of their way to show that they're willing to respect anybody who is."

"Yes, but—!" the marshal began, letting his words trail off as he saw that the other's statement was having its effect on the rest of the audience.

"I'm going out there to attend to a wounded man," Leroy went on. "Not just *one* though. There's likely to be more than him on both sides needing my attention."

"Don't forget that the Wensburys have been taking a licking," warned a supporter of the Maudlins. "They might not be so all fired pleased to act obliging—"

"They will!" Leroy declared, with a complete confidence which brought to an end a protest about to be launched by a Wensbury adherent. "I'll be going out to do what I can for their boss's son. Not that I give a damn about their feelings, or *anybody* else's. All I know is that a wounded man needs my help and I'm going to give it to him."

"And we'll be along to see that you can do it!" Harrigan barked.

"No, Joe!" Leroy contradicted. "Your place—and that of *every* man in this room—is here in town, making sure that the fighting isn't brought in."

"Then let me send for Lil Doc," Damon suggested, knowing and agreeing with the motives behind the other's statement.

"Even if we knew where Josey and the others had taken him on that picnic, there's no time to spare while we send word and he gets back here," Leroy pointed out, having been told that the surprise treat for his son was to take place. "Anyway, this's the last chance he'll have for a fair spell to have some fun with his friends. Let him have it. I'll go alone."

"I'll come with you, Eldridge," Aline Leroy offered. "You'll need help and nobody will try to make trouble for you if I'm along."

None of the audience could dispute the point. All realized that the larger the party and the more men in it, the greater would be the suspicions and disinclination of the warring factions to wait for an explanation before opening fire. That would also be a strong argument against Leroy sending for his son to accompany him. In addition to his well deserved reputation for being capable at assisting on medical matters, he had also acquired a name for being unusually fast and effective with a Colt. Seeing him and remembering his qualities as a gunman it could provoke the response which it was so vitally important to avoid.

"Shall I come with you, Aline?" Mrs. Damon offered and many of the other neutral wives echoed the sentiment.

"There's nothing you could do if you came," Doc's mother replied, being aware that the women would be a pacifying influence where they were. "Eldridge and I can take care of everything that needs doing." Her gaze flickered to the owner of the property which would be their destination. "You might be advised to stay here, Emily."

"Whatever you say, Aline," Widow Simcock answered.

"Where're you going?" Leroy demanded, as Lonny Wensbury started to rise.

"With you," the youngster replied.

"You're *not*!" the doctor stated, knowing that nothing would be more likely to bring trouble upon him than the other's presence. "I can find the Widow's place without needing a guide and I don't need anybody under foot while I'm working."

"But—!" Lonny began.

"So you stay here and nurse your broken head," Leroy finished.

"I don't have no busted head!" Lonny protested, sounding puzzled.

"You *will* have if you give me any more argument," Leroy warned, glancing around the onlookers. "Make sure that he stays here where he'll be safe, Tom Grunwell."

"If you say so, Eldridge," replied the town's lawyer, who was also the youngster's uncle.

"I do," Leroy confirmed. "Let's get going, Aline honey."

About ninety minutes later, Leroy and his wife were riding on the box of the Rocker ambulance towards the unlit clump of buildings on the Widow Simcock's property. There was something of a chill in the air and, to combat it, Aline had donned one of her son's hats and his cloak-coat to cover her dress.

The choice of such masculine attire caused a tragic result!

Fired from the open doors of the barn, as Leroy—having brought the two horse team to a halt—was starting to rise, a bullet ripped into his head. An instant later, in a ragged volley, three more rifles bellowed from close to the position of the first. Only two pieces of the flying lead found their billets in Aline's slender body, but either would have been fatal. Even as her husband crumpled lifeless from the driver's seat, she made an involuntary movement as if trying to stand up. Twisting around, she toppled dying to the ground. Although startled so that they reared and plunged, the two horses were restrained by the vehicle's brakes having been applied and they did not bolt far.

Four shapes emerged from the barn and walked forward. Despite the accuracy with which they had used their weapons, they had the somewhat lurching gait of men who had been drinking.

"Nice shooting, boys," Japhet Maudlin praised, cradling his smoking rifle on the crook of his left arm. "We got both the sons-of-bitches —They're both dead aren't they?"

"They're dead all right," Lazlo Czonka confirmed. "When they go down like *that*, they're wolf-bait for sure, Japhet-boy."

"You called the play right when you said's we shouldn't stop that Wensbury bastard riding to town after we saw him bring his brother in here, Laz," Hank Waltham remarked. "He did go for the Leroys 'n' they come out here alone."

"It was sure slick figuring, Laz," Len Shabber agreed. "And now everybody'll know better'n take sides against your daddy, Japhet."

CHAPTER FOURTEEN

There's Only One Way Out

Taylor Maudlin was no coward, but he quailed before the cold anger being displayed by Hayden Paul Lindrick as they faced each other across the table in the sitting-room of the Lazy M's ranch house. The time was four o'clock in the morning and they had just returned from several hours of strenuous, dangerous activity. Although they had achieved a victory which would end the feud in their favour, there was no signs of jubilation. Nor, tired as they both were, had either the slightest thought of going to sleep.

Already grief-stricken over the death of one son the previous day, Arnold having suffered a relapse and died before Doctor Eldridge Jason Leroy could be summoned, the rancher was now disturbed and guilt-ridden by the information he had received from his boss gun. He was also wondering how he might extricate his youngest son from the consequences of the terrible deed that had been perpetrated on the Widow Simcock's property.

Furiously, Maudlin swung his gaze to where Japhet, Lazlo Czonka, Len Shabber and Hank Waltham were standing by the door. Frightened by the realization of what they had done, the sensation had been increased by the anger and scorn Lindrick had directed upon them when he had found them looking at their murdered victims. Not one of them attempted to meet the rancher's gaze. Much less did any of the quartet want to look at the cold-eyed, stony-featured boss gun.

Having learned that Japhet and the three hired guns had set out in pursuit of Lonny Wensbury, who was helping his wounded brother to escape at the end of the fighting, Lindrick had gone to find them. He had no faith in any of the four's intelligence or good sense, and wanted to prevent them from doing something stupid. On reaching the Widow's place, he found that he was too late. What was more, their stupidity had far exceeded anything he could have anticipated.

The quartet had been staring with horror—even in Czonka's case—over the discovery that they had killed Mrs. Aline Leroy instead of her son. Already the shock had sobered them and they realized just how terrible a deed they had done. If they had hoped to receive comfort, or an attitude of "It can't be helped" from Lindrick, they had rapidly been disillusioned.

One of the reasons Lindrick had been hired as boss by Maudlin was for his experience in conducting the kind of range war in which they were involved. Apart from his personal feelings, which he had had difficulty in controlling, he had been able to foresee the full ramifications and problems that could arise out of the murders. So he had not wasted time in recriminations, although he had left the quartet in no doubts of his feelings for them and their behaviour, but had set about trying to produce a solution to the situation.

Ordering Japhet—who, for once in his life, had shown an almost pathetic eagerness to obey—to go and find his father, but not to mention what had happened in anybody else's hearing, Lindrick had turned his attention to the three hired guns. Learning that Ted Wensbury was dead in the barn, he had made certain arrangements and taken the trio with him to the Lazy M. Arriving shortly before Maudlin, the boss gun had insisted upon an immediate discussion of the matter.

"After all we've done so far, those four stupid sons-of-bitches have just about ruined *everything*!" Lindrick declared, bringing the rancher's attention back to him. None of the others dare even show, much less express, any resentment they might feel over the way he had described them.

"Boone Wensbury's dead and his men scattered to hell and

gone," Maudlin objected, but in a mild fashion. "We've licked them and it's over."

"Like hell it is!" Lindrick contradicted. "You may have licked them with guns, but it's far from over yet—and even more so because of what those four bastards have done. Why do you think I've had you acting the way you have been?"

"How do you mean?" the rancher asked dully, his churning emotions preventing him from thinking clearly.

"Why do you think I had you go into Lampasas to fetch Arnold the way you did and offer to keep your crew out of town when the Wensburys were there?" Lindrick elaborated. "Or why I had you make sure that your men behaved and fixed it so that useless son of yours stopped Waltham from threatening the Leroys? It was to persuade the folks who weren't committed to either side that you aren't such a bad *hombre* and that maybe you'd been pushed into the trouble against your will. And that your family didn't hold it against the Leroys for refusing to take sides. According to your cousin, the lawyer, folks were starting to think that way—and now *this* has happened!"

"I swear to God I didn't know it was Mrs. Le—!" Japhet began, wailed in fact.

"Shut your mouth!" the rancher snarled, his face ashen and rage-distorted as he glared at his son. "If you open it once more, I'll make you wish you'd never been born."

"It's a pity *any* of *them* were born!" Lindrick stated. "But there's nothing we can do to correct *that* now. What we're faced with is how to save the situation. And, as far as I can see, there's only one way out."

"What's that?" Maudlin asked hopefully.

"It'll cost you a fair sum of money," Lindrick warned.

"How much?" the rancher wanted to know, a hint of suspicion in his voice.

"We'll talk about that when you've heard what I intend to do," Lindrick answered.

As he had returned bare-headed to the ranch, the scar like a flattened "W" showed livid and red against the white of his forehead. "Firstly, we can't change the fact that the Leroys are dead. All we can hope to do is turn the blame for it away from your son.

"How?" Maudlin growled, showing his puzzlement and conscious that the other four occupants of the room were listening with bated breath.

"Only the five of us in here know he was involved," Lindrick explained, changing his position so he was facing the quartet by the door. "It was you who told me he'd gone after the Wensbury boys with those three, none of the others had missed him. That's why I sent him straight back to you and told him to keep quiet about what had happened, so if anybody else had arrived before we left, they'd find *me* there and not him. Nobody came, which makes it even easier for you to claim that I was the fourth man, not him."

"*You?*"

"*Me*. We've fixed things back there so it looks as if young Wensbury started shooting as *we* went into the barn, I left my hat with a bullet hole through it, for one thing. For the rest, our story is that, while we was fighting it out with him, the Leroys came dashing up on their ambulance. What *we* told you is that Leroy cut loose at us with his Colt, it's lying by his body with two bullets from it in the door of the barn. So we claimed we began to throw lead back without realizing he had his wife with him."

"Nobody who knows him will believe that Leroy would endanger his wife by acting that way," Maudlin protested.

"*You* didn't think it was likely," Lindrick explained. "Which is why you fired the three of us and told us to get the hell away from your ranch as soon as you heard what we'd done."

"What if Damon wants to know why I didn't hold you for him?" the rancher inquired.

"Who'd be able to do it?" Lindrick countered. "We're the four fastest guns you'd been forced to hire after the *Wensburys* had started bringing them in *first*. Nope. You did all you could by running us out and warning us that if we came back, you'd make a damned good stab at taking us in so our story could be investigated."

"Go on!" Maudlin requested, slumping into a chair.

"That Wensbury boy who was killed on Owl Creek this afternoon started the shooting." Lindrick obliged. "On top of that, you were grieving over Arnold's death, which was caused by him having been bushwhacked by them. You'd even been willing to let that go without bringing in the law. But this was the last straw. When you heard the rest of them were coming, you went to defend your land and turn them back. Nobody can blame you for doing that, or for the fact that somebody got killed in the fighting. It was self defense. Now you've come out the winner, there's not many'll want to argue about it. Most people around here, even those in town who tended to favour the Wensburys, will be too grateful that the feud's over to want to do anything that might keep feelings stirred up. Especially as you'll be saying how bad you feel that it came to shooting and that you don't hold any grudge against the surviving Wensburys and haven't any wish to take any of their land. In fact, you don't even intend to close the 'Fork Range'."

"That's what we intended to do all along," Maudlin pointed out, remembering the plans formulated by his boss gun.

"It was," Lindrick conceded. "But there's the killing of the Leroys for you to take into consideration now. And the only way you'll get by with that is by doing as I've suggested."

Thinking fast, Maudlin considered the boss gun's comments and proposals. The latter had much to recommend them. As Lindrick had said, with his side in the ascendancy, there would have been no danger of repercussions from the local authorities. Wanting an early resumption of normal business and social activities, the weight of public opinion would have been against anything that might tend to prolong the feud. The killing of the doctor and his wife, both well liked and respected members of the community, could arouse such a storm of protest that its ripples would pass beyond the bounds of Lampasas County and might even cause the Governor to instigate an investigation.

However, handled as Lindrick had suggested, it was just possible that—disenchanted by the prospect of further upheavals and a lengthy continuation of the undesirable state of affairs caused by the feud—the population could be willing to let things settle into oblivion.

"We'll do it!" Maudlin decided.

"*Bueno,*" Lindrick replied. "You'll give each of those three five hundred dollars."

"*Five hun—?*" the rancher began.

"For which they'll each sign a confession stating that they and I were the only members of your faction present when the Leroys were killed and it happened in the way I described to you," the boss gun continued, as if the interruption had never happened. "You'll hold the documents and, as soon as they're paid, they'll get the hell as far away from here as they can travel."

"Five hundred dollars *each* you say?" Maudlin asked.

"They'll need it," Lindrick replied, looking at the rancher again and conscious of having the three hired guns' undivided attention. "No matter *whose* idea it was to kill the Leroys, it was murder and *everybody* concerned is equally guilty in the eyes of the law. So they'll hang if they're caught, no matter whether it was your son, or me, who was with them. The money will give them a stake and let them get right out of Texas. It's their only hope of avoiding stretching a rope. Ask them what they think."

"Well?" Maudlin growled, turning his gaze to the trio.

"You give us that money and you won't see us for heel-dust!" Waltham stated, having glanced at the other two and received nods of agreement.

"There's one thing," Lindrick said quietly, swinging towards the three men. "Once you've taken the money and gone, don't *ever* forget that it was *me* with you. If I hear just a hint of anything different, I'll find and kill every one of you without bothering to find out who's responsible."

"Yeah, but—!" Waltham put in, throwing a meaningful and worried look at their employer.

"Don't be any more stupid than you have to!" Lindrick spat out. "Mr. Maudlin can't change the story, even if he wanted to get rid of you that way, without ruining what we're doing it for and putting his son's neck in a noose. Go pack your gear while we write out the documents. Then, as soon as you've signed and been paid, you want to put all the miles you can between yourself and Lampasas County."

"Whatever you say, 'Den,' " grunted Shabber and turned away.

"Sure," Waltham agreed, swinging around to open the door.

For a moment, although he did not offer to meet his employer's or Lindrick's eyes, Czonka hesitated. Then, realizing he would have to raise the objections he was contemplating without the support of his two companions, he slouched out of the room after them.

Snarling a command for his son to go to bed and stay out of his sight, Maudlin watched him leave the room. Then he turned to where Lindrick was drawing up a chair at the table. Producing paper, pens and ink at the boss gun's request, he waited until a copy of the "confession" had been prepared and helped to produce two more.

"Can we trust them even after they've signed these?" the rancher inquired, when the task was completed.

"I'd say 'yes,' " Lindrick replied. "They know that it's the only way they can get enough money to save their hides, because Texas is going to be too hot to hold them when the story gets out."

"What I don't understand is why *you're* doing this," Maudlin declared.

"For money, of course," Lindrick admitted in a matter-of-fact voice. "I'll want fifteen hundred dollars on top of the rest you're paying me for helping you deal with the Wensburys. For that, I'll give you my word—and I've never broken it— that neither you nor young Leroy will ever see or hear from me again."

"Young Leroy?"

"You don't think *he'll* be content to let things go, no matter what anybody else does, do you?"

"I hadn't thought about *him*."

"*I* have," Lindrick stated. "He's going to be looking for the men who killed his parents. And that's one damned good reason why I don't aim to stick around."

"Surely you're faster with a gun than he is?" Maudlin asked.

"I don't know that I am and haven't any wish to find out," Lindrick answered. "One thing I'm sure of, there's not enough difference for either of us to be on our feet if we go up against each other. And another thing is that it sticks in my craw to think how—and why—his parents died. I'm willing to take your money to save that stupid son-of-a-bitch you sired from getting what he deserves, but I won't do anything more that might bring harm or trouble to young Leroy."

"I deserve that and worse," Maudlin conceded. "You might not believe this, Mr. Lindrick, but I'd rather have lost the fight than won if it meant the Leroys were still alive. But it's happened and, worthless as he is, Japhet's my own flesh and blood. So I'll do anything I can to save him. There's *two* thousand over your pay for what you've done and, no matter what you do in the future, I wish you the best in it."

"And I reciprocate it," Lindrick said soberly. "You've earned my respect in the way you're handling this matter. Many a man in your position would have suggested we killed Czonka, Shabber and Waltham instead of paying them off."

"Would that have bothered you?" Maudlin asked.

"Yes," Lindrick replied. "Useless as *they* are, I'd hired them and they'd served you. So I wouldn't have stood for you turning on them to suit your own ends. If you'd suggested doing it, I'd not only have refused, but I'd have pulled out and left you to deal with young Leroy any way you could."

In one respect, it was a pity that Czonka did not hear the final part of the conversation. Having taken the precaution of not unpacking more than the essentials of his belongings, he had completed the gathering of them very quickly. Being of a suspicious nature, he had slipped from the bunkhouse and returned to the main building. Crouching outside the sitting-room window, he had just been in time to hear the comments about the possibility of Doc Leroy wanting to avenge the killings when another of the crew approaching caused him to move away. The idea which had started to form in his mind might have been forgotten if he had been allowed to eavesdrop for a short while longer.

Haggard and inwardly boiling with grief, Doc Leroy walked from his parents' home in the cold grey light of the most terrible morning he had ever known. He looked to where Dirk Damon and several men were standing with rifles or shotguns in their hands. Then he turned his gaze to Rusty Willis. Resting his hands on the porch's rail, the cowhand's normally cheerful face showed how deeply he had been affected by the news that he had brought into town.

On his return from the picnic the previous night, Doc had been told of his parents' departure. Before leaving, his father had left instructions for him to go and make preparations for the work which was likely to be coming in as a result of the fighting. Shortly after one in the morning, the first of the casualties had arrived. Dealing with the three wounded Circle W men, one of whom was seriously wounded, had kept the youngster fully occupied and prevented him from wondering why his mother and father were taking so long. In fact, Rusty had delivered the message from Taylor Maudlin before Doc could ask for somebody to ride out to the Widow Simcock's place and investigate.

Having grown to like and admire the young cowhand, Lindrick had not allowed him to participate in the fighting along Owl Creek. Nor had Rusty particularly wished to do so. Ever since the ambush, he had grown increasingly aware that the feud between the two ranches had gone far beyond acceptable rivalry. He had also become deeply perturbed by the thought that he might find himself compelled to fire on and possibly kill men among whom he had grown up and shared happy hours in the days not too long gone by. So he had not raised any objections when told to stay with the party assigned to help guard the Lazy M's buildings and his employer's womenfolk.

As an aid to the deception he was planning, the first thing Lindrick had done on his return was to send Rusty with the cook and chuckwagon to collect the two dead and three men wounded. When the youngster had come back, he was asked to go into the ranch house. In the sitting-room, looking as shaken as he felt over the disastrous turn of events, Maudlin had told Rusty the story which had been arranged by the boss gun. He had also asked the youngster to deliver the news, along with letters of explanation, to Doc and Dirk Damon.

Furious at learning that Maudlin had been "forced" to let the four hired guns "escape", Rusty never thought to doubt he was being told the truth. Nor did he hesitate over carrying out the far from pleasant task of telling Doc the dreadful news. Riding hard, he was horrified to discover in passing through the Widow Simcock's property, that nobody from the town had found the bodies. It had taken all his courage to go on. Nor could he decide how he might break such tiding to Doc. His final solution was one which he would never have used in less trying circumstances. Visiting Reverend Gazern, he asked for help. A practical man of religion, born and raised in the West, the Reverend had appreciated the youngster's dilemma and accompanied him to the Leroys' home. For all that, it was Rusty who told his friend what had happened.

Never had Doc's medical training, which had given him a deeper insight into life and death than most people ever acquired, stood him in such good stead. Shocked as he was by the news, he refused to let himself become prostrated by grief. Holding his churning emotions in check, he forced himself to read the letter which Rusty had given to him.

Maudlin had written expressing his sympathy and horror at what had happened, explained how he had been "told" the incident had taken place and, without trying to avoid at least part of the responsibility, had hoped that Doc would go to the Lazy M ranch house to treat the wounded men. On learning that they were cowhands who he knew as friends, the youngster had decided to do so. However, at the Reverend's insistence, he had waited until his parents' bodies had been collected and brought home. He had just finished making the arrangements for their funerals and was ready to set out for the Lazy M.

"Everything points to it happening as Maudlin was told,"

Damon announced, having received similar information from the rancher. "Except that I can't believe your father would behave as Lindrick claimed."

"So Lindrick *was* there!" Doc said, half to himself, walking to where his horse was saddled and waiting.

"We found his hat in the barn," Damon admitted, for he too had been puzzled by the boss gun having been blamed. It had not struck him as the kind of thing Lindrick would do. "Anyways, we're going with you to see Maudlin."

"No you're *not*!" Doc contradicted firmly, starting to fasten his father's medical bag to the horse's saddlehorn. "That would be asking for trouble. And, if you all come, there'll be nobody left to make sure the town stays peaceable."

"You're right on both counts," Damon conceded. "But you're not going alone. Nobody's taken my country sheriff's badge away from me, so I'm putting it on and riding with you. Joe Harrigan's acting as town marshal while I'm away and he'll take care of things here."

"I'm coming too," Rusty declared. "I'm quitting the Lazy M and have to fetch my gear. So I might's well do it n—"

At that moment, a rider appeared from between two of the buildings along the opposite side of the street. Revolver in hand, he sent his horse racing towards the group of men.

One glance, even as startled yells rose from the crowd, warned Doc of his peril. Recognizing Lazlo Czonka, one of the men named as being responsible for his parents' death, he could guess that his own life was endangered.

And it was!

Remembering what he had overheard about the possibility of Doc seeking vengenace, Czonka had also been mindful of the youngster's deadly ability with a gun. So he had parted company with his companions and made for Lampasas with the intention of removing the menace. It had been his hope that he would find his would-be victim alone and in such a state of grief as to be unable to resist. Instead, from all appearances, the youngster was preparing to ride with a posse and there could only be one reason for it having been formed. They were almost certain to be going out to hunt down the quartet.

Deciding that the best way to handle the situation was throw a scare into the townsmen and kill the youngster, Czonka was charging into the attack.

Taken unawares, all but one person in the crowd were too amazed to respond.

Hurling himself away from the others and towards the centre of the street, Doc drew all of Czonka's attention to himself. Flame gushed from the revolver in the hired gun's fist even as Doc's Colt was clearing leather. Passing lead caused the air to fan against the youngster's cheek. Instead of halting and presenting his assailant with a stationary target, he made a rolling dive onwards. As it ended, his own weapon slanted upwards and bellowed. He missed his intended mark, but his purpose was still served.

Hit in the head, Czonka's horse started to collapse beneath him. Throwing himself clear, he contrived to alight on his feet—for all the good it did him.

Five times, as swiftly as he could work the hammer and control the recoil, Doc sent bullets into the hired gun's chest. Czonka was driven backwards by the impacts. With his body torn to doll rags, he crashed lifeless on to the wheel-rutted surface of the street.

CHAPTER FIFTEEN

Kill Me and You've Killed *Him* Too

Japhet Maudlin should never have been on the porch of the ranch house when Doc Leroy arrived at the Lazy M ranch house accompanied by Rusty Willis and Dirk Damon.

Although Japhet had obeyed his father's order and retired to his room, sleep refused to come and he had spent several restless hours brooding over his situation. In spite of feeling sure that his father would shield him from the consequences of his part in the killing of Doctor and Mrs. Leroy, he was in a state of apprehension. Memories of how fast and deadly with a gun he knew his victims' son to be kept haunting him. By the time his father had come in and told him of the arrangements that had been made for his salvation, his hatred of Doc Leroy had increased to the point where he had not cared about anything else. Certainly he had been devoid of gratitude for the reprieve his father's money had purchased for him.

Such was Japhet's nature that he had come to consider himself innocent of any part in the killings. However, at the back of his mind had lurked a warning that something might go wrong. If that happened, Doc Leroy would learn the truth and want revenge. Japhet was all too aware of just how little chance he would have in a fair fight, either with guns or bare-handed, against the pallid-faced son of his victims. Far from intelligent, he had drawn a conclusion. Leroy must killed *before* learning the truth. The main problem had been how to

156

bring such a desirable result about. Hearing that the other had been asked to visit the ranch suggested that an opportunity to do so might be arranged.

It had seemed to Japhet that luck was favouring him. Shortly after dawn, the San Saba lawyer had arrived with a request that Taylor Maudlin should go to meet and make peace with Mrs. Wensbury. Remembering the advice given by Hayden Paul Lindrick on the benefit of showing willingness to bring about a cessation of hostility, the rancher had agreed that he, his wife and sister would go. Doing so had left Frank, the oldest brother, in command at the ranch, and he was unaware of Japhet's participation in the killings in the Widow Simcock's barn.

Knowing his brother to be quick tempered and protective where he was concerned, Japhet had felt sure that some solution to his problem could be arranged. Nor did the fact that Doc had two men with him cause him to revise his plans. As far as he knew, Rusty was still a loyal Lazy M hand. Failing to notice that Damon was wearing the sheriff's five-pointed star and not the shield-shaped badge of the town marshal, he felt he could dismiss the peace officer as a relevant factor. Everybody present remembered how Damon had disarmed Lindrick's party on the night of the ambush and, although he had put the men responsible for it in jail, he had accepted the pack of lies they had told and set them free. So they would not harbour friendly feelings where he was concerned.

"It's about time you got here!" Japhet barked, striding down the porch's steps to where, having dismounted, his would-be victim was about to unstrap the medical bag. "I suppose you've been too busy tending to them stinking Wensburys to care if our boys lived or died."

Leaving the bag, Doc swung towards the speaker. Cold anger boiled through him, but he managed to hold it in check. One factor leapt to his notice. Although Frank Maudlin and the half a dozen hard faced men who were gathering around had on their gunbelts, Japhet was unarmed.

"Where are they, Frank?" Doc asked, looking towards the older brother.

"*I'm* talking to you!" Japhet yelled, leaping forward to

catch hold of the visitor's arm. "Don't come the high-toned doctor with—"

Feeling the other's touch, all the flood-gates of Doc's pent-up emotions erupted. Swinging around and snatching his arm free, he caught the front of Japhet's shirt with both hands. Fury gave an added strength to his wiry body and, with a surging heave, he flung his antagonist away from him.

Taken completely unprepared, Japhet was sent reeling on uncontrollable legs. Catching one against the other, he tripped. Before he, or anybody else, could make a move to prevent it, he plunged head first and with a sickening impact against the upright support of the porch. Bouncing from it, he collapsed to sprawl limp and motionless on the wooden steps.

"What the—?" Damon began, his right hand moving towards the butt of the Adams.

"Stand still, Dirk!" Frank Maudlin advised, jerking a thumb to where two men were lining rifles from the front windows of the ranch house. "You're covered!"

"Hey!" Rusty yelled, glaring around. "What the hell's this?"

"You keep your hand clear as well, cow nurse!" ordered one of the hired guns, drawing his revolver and lining at the red-haired youngster. "You're a whole heap too friendly with these two to be trusted."

Having delivered his warning and seen it obeyed, Frank hurried towards his brother. Kneeling, he looked down for a moment. Then he swung an angry face towards the author of Japhet's misfortunes.

"Get over here and take a look at him!" Frank snarled.

"Go to hell!" Doc answered flatly, but conscious that one of the rifles was pointing straight at his head.

Thrusting erect, Frank jerked the Colt from his holster. Although he was unaware of the true facts, he had heard about Doc's parents having been killed. So he had taken precautions in case the youngster arrived at the ranch seeking revenge rather than to render aid to the wounded. Instead of considering the way in which his brother had behaved, he was drawing entirely the wrong conclusions from the situation.

Like Doc, Frank was suffering under a great strain. Up

until the previous evening, he had never realized the full implications of a feud. Badly shaken by the killings and injuries that had taken place, he still was not thinking with anything close to his usual sensibility. There was, however, more behind his reaction than that.

Sharing his father's guilty conscience over the deaths of Doc's parents, he had misread the other's motives in hurling Japhet away. Attributing the action as being provoked by a desire to take vengeance, the protective feelings he had where his youngest brother was concerned drove every rational thought from his head.

"I said get over here!" Frank snarled and the Colt trembled in his grasp with the rage that filled him. "Do it, or I'll kill you where you stand."

"Kill me and you've killed *him* too, most likely," Doc answered, once again mastering his emotions and appreciating the deadly peril facing not only himself but his companions. "So, happen you're that way inclined, go ahead."

"Maybe you'd rather see one of your *amigos* shot?" suggested a hired gun.

"You're making a damned fool mistake, Frank!" Damon warned.

"Like hell I am!" Maudlin snarled. "If he's killed Japhet, or the kid dies because of this, I'll kill him!"

"Have him taken inside," Doc ordered. "I'll look him over when I've seen the rest of your woun—"

"You'll see to him right now!" Frank raged, his hot temper close to breaking point.

"Best do it, *amigo*," Rusty advised. "Mrs. Maudlin and Miss Beth saw to the fellers and they won't take no hurt for a while longer."

Already Doc's instincts were suggesting that he should at least examine Japhet. He had heard the sickening crunch with which the other's head had met the porch's sturdy supporting rail and knew all too well how serious such a collision could be. In addition, he knew that he could not press Frank's patience much further. With his nerves stretched almost to breaking point, the young man might do something for which he would be sorry later. Furthermore, if he pulled the Colt's trigger, the hired guns would not be willing to allow two witnesses—Rusty and Damon—to the cold blooded killing to live and tell about it.

"All right," Doc said quietly. "I'll see to him."

"Shed that gunbelt first!" Frank commanded.

"That goes for you pair's well!" supplemented the man who had taken Lindrick's place as boss gun.

Knowing that to refuse would avail them nothing, Doc, Rusty and Damon obeyed. Having unbuckled and hung his gunbelt over the saddlehorn, Doc liberated his father's medical bag. Ignoring the hostile way in which Frank and the hired guns were regarding him, he crossed to the porch. Only a brief examination was needed to warn him that *very* skilled attention was required. Every symptom served to confirm what he had suspected.

"His skull's fractured," Doc announced, straightening up. "I can't do anything—"

"*Can't,* or *won't?*" Frank spat out.

"Can't," Doc repeated. "It's like that time one of your hands was kicked in the head by his horse—"

"You helped your daddy to save *him*!" Frank pointed out.

"Yes, but—," Doc began.

"There's no son-of-a-bitching '*but*' about it!" Frank ejaculated, remembering all the stories he had heard about the youngster's knowledge and ability in performing medical and surgical tasks. "You can do the same for Japhet."

"Don't be *loco*!" Doc shouted back, having to fight to hold his temper in check. "I haven't the gear—"

"Then we'll have it fetched for you!" Frank interrupted.

"By the time it gets here, it'll be too late," Doc objected, forcing himself to think.

"Then, by God, I'll kill you to be even for him!" Frank threatened.

Already Doc's instinct to heal was overriding his resentment of such treatment and driving him to consider how he might save Japhet's life. However, Frank's words gave him an added inducement. In his present frame of mind, the rancher's son would not hesitate to carry out the threat. Not only would he kill Doc, but the same fate would descend upon Rusty and Damon as soon as it happened.

From his training, the youngster knew that there was only one way to prevent the injury from killing Japhet. Unless the pressure caused to the brain by the fractured skull was relieved, he would die.

Doc knew what to do. Not only had he helped his father to treat the cowhand suffering from a similar injury, he had successfully carried out trephining operations on animals and upon the skull of a human skeleton the doctor had purchased from a medical supply house in the East.

The only problem was that, although he had everything else he would need in his father's medical bag to perform the operation, Doc had not thought to include the cylindrical trephine saw with which to cut away the fragment of bone.

Three lives, apart from Japhet's, hung in the balance because of the omission!

There was no way—

"Quick!" Doc snapped, thoughts churning through his head. "Go and fetch me a thimble from your momma's sewing basket and—"

"A *thimble*?" Frank gasped, his revolver wavering for a moment. Then anger creased his face and he went on, "If this's a—"

"It's your brother's life that's at stake, god damn it!" Doc blazed. "Get me the thimble, a feather duster or something with a handle like it and a shingle nail."

"A-A-A—?" Frank gobbled, staring as if unable to believe his ears.

"A new nail, not one that's rusted! Doc continued. "Move it, blast you. There's little enough time as it is."

"Come on!" Rusty Willis yelled, striding forward without a thought for the risk he was taking. Nor did he know what his *amigo* had in mind, but was willing to give all his support to it. "I'll help you fetch 'em, Frank."

"Best make it *two* of each, it'll save time if a second's needed," Doc corrected as the pair passed him on their way to the front door. "And I'd like them afore fall."

"Yo!" Rusty responded, disappearing into the building.

"Don't you try any tricks!" Frank warned, pausing on the threshold.

"Four of you come and help me take Japhet indoors," Doc barked at the onlookers, ignoring the comment. "You'd best be one of them, Dirk. I want at least *one* of the carriers to have the sense of a seam-squirrel."

Under the urging of the vitriolic-tongued youngster, Damon obtained the requisite assistants to lift and carry the unconscious Japhet into the house. Having been there as a guest in happier times, Doc knew where he would find the best location for the work that lay ahead. There was a momentary hesitation on the part of the hired guns when they heard where they were to go. However, Damon brought it to an end. Taking their burden into the sitting-room, they waited until the youngster had cleared the table and covered it with sheets of clean newspaper, then laid Japhet on it.

"Here're the thimble and dusters, Doc!" Rusty announced, running in with the objects. "Frank's going to the barn for the shingle nails."

"Go with him, Dirk," Doc requested, although the words were closer to a command. "Take the thimbles and dusters. Work on one set at a time. First off, cut some real sharp little teeth around the rim of the thimble. Fasten it on to the end of the duster's handle here, then cut off and make a sharp point on the nail so it just shows beyond the thimble's rim."

"Whatever you say," Damon promised, after a few seconds while he was committing the instructions to his memory.

"Hey, Hambone!" Doc said, seeing the ranch's cook in the doorway. "Come in here and lend me a hand. The rest of you get the hell outside and keep quiet!"

"Don't you pull anything," growled the new boss gun. "We're keeping your *amigo* where it'll—"

"Do what the hell you've a mind!" Doc snarled. "Only do it well clear of *this* blasted room." Turning his back on the man, he looked at the cook and went on, "I'll want him stripped to the waist and the part of his head I'll be working on shaved."

"Sure, young feller," Hambone answered, then directed a

baleful glare at the onlookers. "You heard him. Get the hell away from here."

"*You* stay with *us*!" the new boss gun ordered Rusty.

"Sure," the youngster replied, oozing disdain. "And, happen you're scared, I'll hold your itty-bitty hand."

"*Hombre!*" Doc barked, looking up as the boss gun let out an obscene oath. "Happen anything comes off to Rusty, you'll *not* be helping Japhet's chances."

Waiting with small patience until he and the cook had been left by the other men, Doc set to work. They did not waste time in talking. For all that, they had only just completed the preparations when Damon returned. Looking worried, puzzled and suspicious, Frank followed.

"I hope this is all right," the sheriff said, handing over the device he had manufactured.

"It looks as if it might be," Doc answered, examining the extemporized trephine saw. The head of the duster had been removed and he tested the security of the thimble attached to the end of the handle. Satisfied on that score, he checked the teeth which had been cut around the rim and the amount the point of the nail was protruding. "It'll do fine."

"I've got Daybreak making the other one," Damon replied.

"Have him finish it and make sure everything's as good as this," Doc requested.

"Are you saying you're going to use *that* thing on Japhet?" Frank demanded.

"I didn't have it made to hook the shit out of my arse," Doc answered.

"God damn it!" Frank almost bellowed. "If this's a trick—"

"I know," Doc sighed. "You'll kill me. Happen you're set on doing it, go ahead. Only, like I told you before, kill me and you've killed Japhet as well."

"All right!" Frank hissed. "Do what you're fixing to. But you've got my word that I meant it when I said I'll kill you if he doesn't pull through."

"You ain't helping keep him alive none, Frank-boy," put in the cook, an old retainer who had privileges that would not have been accorded to anybody else. "And I don't take it kind, nor friendly, happen you reckon's *I'd* let young Leroy do whatever he's fixing to happen I wasn't certain sure it'd be for the best."

"Come on, Frank," Damon supplemented. "Let's leave them to their work. Neither Rusty nor I'll make fuss for you while they're doing it."

"What now, young feller?" Hambone asked, watching the two men take their departure.

"I'm going to what they call 'sterilize' this contraption in that stuff I've got boiling on the hob," Doc explained, indicating a steaming saucepan resting on the projecting ledge which was fitted at the side of the fireplace to keep such utensils warm. In it was a solution of bichloride of mercury that he had taken from the medical bag without allowing the cook an opportunity to see the other contents. "Then we'll see if I can save Japhet's life."

"I hope you can," Hambone declared soberly. "I've never seen Frank so all-fired mean, ornery and hawg-wild. Happen young Japhet here cashes in, he's just riled enough to do what he says."

Completing the sterilization of his implements, his father having been an early convert to such a vitally important precaution, Doc returned to the table. Much to his relief, he could see no sign of his patient recovering consciousness. Using the tip of the nail to centre the home-made instrument on the section of the skull which he had to incise, he commenced the trephining operation.

Taylor Maudlin, his wife and sister returned before Doc had completed his task, but he paid them not the slightest attention. Nor, seeing how far he had progressed, did they offer to interfere.

An hour had gone by. During it, Damon and Rusty had never been allowed out of the hired guns' sight. Nor, as the sheriff had promised, did they offer to cause any disturbance. They were, however, relieved when the rancher's party arrived. For all that, the vigilance continued.

At last, the front door opened.

Carrying his father's medical bag, Doc walked out of the house and came to a stop on the porch. Silence fell over the grim-faced crowd who were hovering in front of the building and guarding the two hostages. They realized that the operation had come to an end and waited to be told its result.

"I've taken out the piece of bone and relieved the pressure on his brain like I promised," the pallid-faced youngster informed them. "Now Rusty, Dirk Damon and I are going back to Lampasas."

"Give them their guns and let them go," Maudlin authorized, from the doorway. "He's done what he promised and Japhet's going to live."

"By god, *amigo*, you're the cool one!" Rusty breathed, as they went towards their waiting horses. "Or did you reckon Frank was only making wind-talk when he said he'd kill you if Japhet died?"

"I *knew* he meant it," Doc declared.

"Didn't that worry you?" Damon asked.

"Not over much," Doc said quietly, lifting the medical bag in his right hand and which had been close to him all the time he was operating. "My daddy always kept a loaded and capped Army Colt in here. It's still inside—and, if Japhet had been dying, *I'd* have known before anybody else."

PART THREE

Doc's Dilemma

CHAPTER SIXTEEN

Ole Devil's Dead

"Japhet Maudlin recovered, but I could have saved my time, he was killed a year later while he was trying to hooraw Abilene," Doc Leroy told Doctor Alphonse Jules Dumoulin. "Rusty Willis and Joe Brambile went with me when I took out after Lindrick and the other two hired guns. We trailed them down towards Trinity, but a few miles out of town, we came across a share-cropper's place and his wife was in labour. Not the easy way, either. When I examined her, I could see that she'd need a Caesarean[1] and damned near straight away if it was going to be any use. There wouldn't be time to fetch out a doctor. So Joe and Rusty rode on while I stopped to do it. They ran across Len Shabber and Hank Waltham and when the smoke cleared, had made wolf-bait out of them. Trouble was, they died without talking and Lindrick wasn't with them. I never did find out where he'd gone, nor hear anything of him until I took his brace of fancy Colt Pocket Pistols from that yahoo in the bank."

"I see," the dean of the Soniat Memorial-Mercy Hospital's Medical College said quietly. "And what happened to the share-cropper's wife?"

1. Caesarean operation: the delivery of a baby via a section of the abdominal walls and the womb of the mother when an ordinary birth is apparently impossible. Said to have gained its name through having been necessary at the birth of Julius Caesar.

"She had a right smart little son, ten—well, eight anyways—pounds," Doc replied.

"I always say the first baby I delivered weighed *twelve* pounds," Dumoulin stated with a frosty smile. "But I suspect it was closer to—er—nine."

"At the least nine, sir," Doc grinned.

"Thank you. Is searching for Lindrick why you didn't come and commence your education?"

"Not all the way, sir. Joe made me give up the hunt after about six months. When I got back home, I learned that daddy had been a heap better doctor than a businessman. He'd left a whole stack of debts, mostly to folks who needed the money. So I stayed on, went to work for Stone Hart's Wedge trail crew with Rusty and earned enough to pay everybody off. Time I'd done it, well there was first one thing and then another. So I never got around to coming."

"But you obviously kept up your studies," Dumoulin declared.

"Yes, sir," Doc agreed. "I bought and read everything I could lay my hands on, talked to and worked with doctors all I could. There were times when knowing about medicine, or surgery, came in real handy."

"Tell me about them," the dean requested.

Knowing his future career was in the balance, Doc concluded it was no time for false modesty. So he gave Dumoulin examples of how he had made use of his knowledge by treating illnesses and coping with the accidents or other mishaps which had occurred during the years since the death of his parents. He mentioned how he had removed a bullet to save Waco's life,[2] described the part he had played in controlling an outbreak of typhoid in Canvastown,[3] Arizona and the way he had coped with the delivery of twins to the wife of a now famous entertainer,[4] among other things. He also brought a brief smile to the Dean's face when mentioning a comment

---

2. Told in: *Return To Backsight*.
3. Told in Case Five "Statute of Limitations" of: *Sagebrush Sleuth*.
4. Told in the "The Juggler and the Lady" episode of: *Waco Rides In*.

made by an Irish cavalry sergeant who had heard him talking about the need for a doctor to understand Latin.

"Sure and I don't see what's the need," the gallant Sergeant Magoon had declared. "You're never likely to meet one of them Latins to need to speak to."[5]

"I understand that you helped Doctor Bieler carry out an appendectomy a few days ago," Dumoulin remarked, at the end of the young man's recital. "He was most impressed by your knowledge."

"It wasn't the first excision of the vermiform appendix I'd come across, sir," Doc replied.

"You'd witnessed a similar operation?" Dumoulin asked, for in the early 1880's the appendectomy was far from the comparatively simple operation it would eventually become with the aid of improved equipment, drugs and techniques.

"Not so much 'witnessed' as done, sir," Doc corrected and told how he had been compelled to operate when one of the Wedge cowhands had burst his appendix during a trail drive far from any hope of qualified assistance. "Only it's *not* true I cut it out with a bowie knife, which I've heard tell the boys claim. I used my daddy's instruments."

"Which doesn't lessen your achievement, young man," the Dean declared, then his gaze went to the two newspapers on the desk. "However, we have something else to consider. I can understand now why you felt you had to find and question the man with Lindrick's revolvers. But that won't have any weight where the *Intelligencer* is concerned. Rather the opposite, in fact. They'll want to know by whose authority you were allowed to conduct a personal vendetta—which is how they'll chose to regard it—under the protection of the New Orlean's Police Department."

"I reckon they will, sir," Doc admitted, being aware of the virulence shown by "liberal" newspapers such as the *New Or-*

5. Sergeant Magoon appears in: *The Rushers* and *Apache Rampage*. Due to an error in the documents from which the author obtained the facts of the story, he is referred to as "Muldoon" in *Trouble Trail* of the *Calamity Jane* series. J.T.E.

leans Intelligencer where the forces of law and order were concerned. "They'll likely try to rub cow dung on the College and Hospital as well if it will help them to get at me."

"Undoubtedly. There are those here who the *Intelligencer* would be only too delighted to bring down and something like this could open the way."

"That being the case, sir, the best thing for all concerned will be for me to resign from the College, pull up my stakes and head for home."

Just as Doc finished making his suggestion, there was a knock at the door. Frowning, Dumoulin called for the person to come in. It opened to admit his secretary. Much to the Texan's surprise, he saw his wife behind the man. One glance at her face as she entered told him that she was deeply troubled.

"Mrs. Leroy has brought a telegraph message for her husband, sir," the secretary announced. "It's contents are such that I felt he should see them without delay."

"Here, Doc," Lynn Leroy said, hurrying forward and holding out a buff coloured Western Union message form. Her voice was husky as she went on, "It's—It's—"

"Easy, honey!" Doc said, alarmed by the display of emotion from his usually self controlled young wife. He had risen at the sight of her and, taking the sheet of paper, lowered her on to his vacated seat. "Are you all right?"

"Y-Yes," Lynn replied. "Th-The message—!"

"Oh my Lord!" Doc ejaculated, opening and reading the neatly printed writing of a Western Union telegraph operator. "Ole Devil's dead!"

Taking the paper from the Texan's limp fingers, Dumoulin stared at it.

> *"Doc,*
> *It is with deepest regret that I have to inform you Uncle Devil passed away peacefully in his sleep last night. We realize that you cannot attend the funeral, but felt that you would wish to be informed.*
>
> *Dusty Fog."*

Letting the paper slip from his hand, Dumoulin sat as if turned to stone. Like Doc, he was staring blankly ahead of him. Each was thinking of Jackson Baines Hardin, but they were regarding him in vastly different lights.

To Doc, it was General Hardin he called to mind. His employer, whose stern and hard exterior had covered a kindness and sense of humour. Who had always been willing to come to the aid of a friend, or serve the best interests of Texas and, although his disability would not allow him to help personally, would send his very capable floating outfit[6] to act on his behalf.

Instead of thinking of Ole Devil as an elderly man, Dumoulin's recollection was of a fateful day in Texas when he had looked through the smoke of a shot with the horrifying realization that he had missed. Confronting him, the tall, ramrod straight figure had hirsute adornment so shaped as to give its features a Mephistophelian aspect which went so well with the name "Ole Devil". He was sighting the barrel of a steady rock-held pistol at Dumoulin. However, no bullet had winged its way into his body. Despite having been narrowly missed by young Dumoulin's shot, Ole Devil had declined to reply in kind.

The refusal, made in a way that did not offend or affect Dumoulin's honour, was something he had never forgotten. It had left him in Ole Devil's debt, but that had not been mentioned in the letter written years later about the young man who now stood on the other side of his desk. Instead, Ole Devil had written about many of the incidents which he had just heard at first hand, and had recommended that Marvin Eldridge Leroy should be enrolled as a student and given an opportunity to qualify as a doctor.

Almost two minutes went by in silence.

6. In the open range days, the large ranches employed four to six men to work the more distant areas of their spreads as a "floating outfit". Ole Devil frequently dispatched his as trouble-shooters to assist friends who were in difficulties.

Dumoulin was the first to break it.

Thinking of what he owed to Ole Devil Hardin, he had reached a decision.

"Mr. Leroy," the Dean said. "Do you think that you could sit for your qualifying examination next Monday?"

For a moment, Doc could not believe his ears. Then he realized the chance that he was being offered.

"Yes, sir," Doc said and felt Lynn grip his hand in a grasp that hurt. "I can."

"Then you will," Dumoulin promised. "And, if you pass, you'll leave New Orleans as a qualified doctor."

CHAPTER SEVENTEEN

You Have To Keep
Haynes Lashricker Alive

"Sure, I know Haynes Lashricker, Doctor," the conductor of the train bound for Keaton stated, leaning against the back of the seat occupied by Lynn and Doc Leroy. "Is he a friend of your'n?"

On the luggage rack above the young couple, in addition to their hats, was a new black leather medical bag clearly inscribed with gold letters:

"Dr. M.E. LEROY, M.D."

Making good on the offer he had presented, Doctor Alphonse Jules Dumoulin had arranged for Doc to take his qualifying examination prematurely. No other favouritism had been shown and it had been upon his own merits that he had passed with honours. Having achieved his goal, he had kept the promise he had made. He and his wife were on their way to the West before the *New Orleans Intelligencer* was aware of what had taken place.

Even before they had left the riverboat and boarded the trans-continental train, Lynn had known that Doc was intending to pay a visit to the town in which he had been told Hayden Paul Lindrick was living under the same name of "Haynes Lashricker". In fact, the decision to do so had been as much hers as his. Furthermore, on her own initiative, she had persuaded Captain Phillipe St. Andre of the New Orleans Police Department to turn over the matched brace of Colt Pocket Pistols to her husband so that he could return them to their owner.

Neither of the young couple could visualize what might transpire from the delivery of the pistols to their rightful owner. Nor did they try to decide what Doc would do when he met the man who had been blamed for the killing of his parents. However, each had known that he would never rest easily until it had been done.

Having transferred to a smaller and less comfortable local train, Lynn and Doc were now traversing the spur line in the direction of the Colorado-Wyoming border. In another hour at the most, they would reach their destination.

Wanting to know more about the man they were going far out of their way to meet, they had engaged the conductor in conversation. They had been helped in this by the evidence of Doc's profession. While the bag might be new, he was obviously older and more mature than would have been the case with the average person who had qualified so recently. What was more, as his hat and attire proved, he was anything but a dude freshly arrived from the pampered East.

Having suggested a possible cure for the railroad official's rheumatism and made a couple of jokes about the use of whiskey in the treatment of snake-bites—with references to the advisability of always carrying one's private snake to provide the need for the cure—Doc had gradually brought up the subject which was of greatest interest to him. A casual question while they were discussing the right-of-way trouble began to produce the desired results.

"No, I can't say that we've ever met," Doc admitted frankly, the conductor's tone and attitude suggesting that he thoroughly approved of the man they were discussing. "But I've heard a few things about him."

"*What* you've heard likely depends on *who* was doing the telling," the conductor remarked dryly, studying the young Texan with appraising eyes.

"You could say that about "most everybody," Doc pointed out, speaking in a lighter fashion than he was feeling. "Why there's even folks who say that Wyatt Earp was a mean, ornery, dishonest son-of-a—gentleman.' "

"Wyatt Earp *is* a mean, ornery, whateveryou was going to call him," the conductor stated. "But, no matter what you might've heard tell, Haynes Lashricker's a damned fine man. And I'm not saying that just 'cause I'm working for the railroad. If it hadn't been for him, this whole damned—pardon me for such words, ma'am—section'd've gone up in gunsmoke afore now."

"Like I told you, we've been down in New Orleans for a fair spell," Doc said soothingly. "All we've heard is some talk, but not much, except that Haynes Lashricker was a name that kept cropping up."

"It likely would," the railroad official conceded, sounding mollified. "When he was sent out here from the head office back East, we figured he'd be nothing more'n another shiny-butted desk warmer. Was *we* surprised. He took over when things was all set to pop and cooled them down."

For the remainder of the journey, Doc was granted an insight into the way that Lindrick—if, indeed, he was "Lashricker"—had handled a very delicate and potentially dangerous situation. What was more, he felt sure that the hard-bitten old conductor's respect and high regard was genuine and did not stem from purely partisan feelings. Yet there was no suggestion that Lindrick had acted in his old capacity as boss gun. For all that, he had kept the railroad's professional fighting men under control and ruled them with the same iron hand that had been in evidence during the "Fork Range" war back in Lampasas County, Texas. Through his efforts alone, unless the official was exaggerating, there had been none of the bloodshed and violence that had marked disputes of a similar nature in other parts of the country.

At last, with the train slowing for its stop at Kenton, the conductor went to attend to his duties. Taking their hats and Doc's bag from the luggage rack, the couple went to stand on the entrance platform. Looking ahead, Doc's gaze picked out two people among the small crowd waiting at the depot. One was a tall, wide shouldered, blond haired and handsome young man in the attire of a Texas cowhand and with a brace of matched staghorn handled Colt Artillery Model Peacemakers in the tied down holsters of an exceptionally well designed and made gunbelt. Apart from the clothing being different and the black hair being longer, the woman at his side might have been Lynn.

"It's Beth and Waco!" Doc ejaculated, then swung an accusing gaze to his wife. "Now *how* do *you* reckon *they* knew *we'd* be coming *here*?"

"Why isn't that *kind* of them?" Lynn said, oozing innocence. "Of course, it's what I'd expect from *our* side of the family. A girl should *always* be met by her loving sister when she's coming home from a long visit."

"This *isn't* coming home for *us*," Doc protested. "And I don't believe in fortune telling."

"Well—," Lynn purred. "It could just be that I might have mentioned we'd be coming home through Kenton—and when—in that telegraph message I sent to them."

"That's about what I figured," Doc declared and gave his wife's right bicep a gentle squeeze. "*Gracias*, honey."

However, there was no time to be spent on lengthy and warm greetings, or in explaining why Lynn had sent the message asking for her sister and brother-in-law to come to Kenton and meet them.

"Thank the Good Lord you're on this train, *amigo*!" Waco declared fervently, as he and Doc were shaking hands and the sisters embracing. "Have you brought all your doctoring gear along?"

"What's not in the bag here's with the rest of our gear in the caboose," Doc replied, realizing that only a serious emergency would produce such behaviour from the very capable young sheriff of Two Forks County. "What's up?"

"There's something real important for you to do," Waco answered. "You have to keep Haynes Lashricker alive."

"*Haynes Lash*—!" Doc ejaculated and, hearing the words as she was turning to greet her brother-in-law, Lynn gave a gasp.

"He's taken *real* sick," Waco elaborated, puzzled by the response to the name he had mentioned. "It's just like that feller when we were working for the Hashknife Outfit, the one you and the doctor from Bisbee had to cut open."

"Appendicitis!" Doc growled, remembering the incident as being the second occasion when he had participated in such an operation.

"*Acute* appendicitis, Doc," Lynn's sister put in. "I couldn't be sure, but I think it won't be long before it bursts."

"So far, we've stopped anybody from learning he's ill," Waco went on, knowing his wife had studied enough about medical matters to have made an accurate diagnosis. "But, if he dies, this whole damned section could blow apart at the seams. There's not much time to spare, *amigo*."

"You don't know what you're asking him to do, Waco!" Lynn gasped. "Lashricker might be the man who killed his mother and father!"

"Lindrick?" Waco growled, for he had heard of how Doc's parents had died. "Are you *sure* of it, *amigo*?"

"Everything points that way," Doc stated, emotions churning through him.

The four young people had moved away from the train. Standing in a rough diamond-shape, they were all experiencing a sense of strain over the unexpected development.

"I noticed the scar on his forehead," Waco admitted. "But it never occured to me that—He sure's hell isn't a hired gun now, *amigo*. From what Dan Troop—he's town marshal up here—told me and I've seen for myself, I've taken him for one damned fine *hombre*."

"We're staying with him and his wife," Beth went on and her face showed an even deeper distress. "Oh Lord. They've invited you, too."

"Did they know that it was *me* who'd be coming?" Doc demanded.

"Yes," Beth confirmed. "It was Hay—Lin—Hay—he who suggested that you should be their guests."

"When I saw what was ailing him and remembered you'd be here in the afternoon train, I thought everything would work out fine," Waco said slowly. "But now—"

"We're with you on *whatever* you decide, Doc," Beth declared and her husband nodded in agreement.

For a full two minutes, Doc made no reply. He stood like a

statue and with only his eyes betraying the inner turmoil he was experiencing. Two different sensations were warring inside him; bitterness over the thought of how his parents were murdered and the memory of his recently taken Hippocratic oath.[1] He had never taken lightly his duties in the healing field and even less so since he had received his degree as a Doctor of Medicine.

Knowing what conflicts he must be enduring, neither Doc's wife, her sister, nor his very close friend offered to speak and influence his decision. In spite of all he had learned about the way in which Lashricker—or Lindrick—was containing a highly explosive situation, Waco refused to make any suggestions to the man whose skill as a surgeon had on one occasion saved him from death. It was, the young peace officer appreciated, something which Doc must face alone.

At last, a shudder shook the pallid-faced young man and he stiffened as it ended.

"Have our gear brought to the Lashrickers' place, Waco!" Doc requested and his voice held the commanding note which always came into it when he was about to commence a medical or surgical chore. "Lynn, Beth, I can't do any appendectomy on my own. I'm going to need help."

"You've got it," Beth promised without hesitation and, too full of her emotions to speak, Lynn nodded.

"There's one thing, though," Doc went on, eyeing the sisters in a warning manner. "What you'll be seeing won't be pretty. So, happen you *have* to swoon, fall backwards and not *across* the patient."

"That's my husband!" Lynn Leroy ejaculated, slapping her thighs in mock exasperation, watching Doc striding away in the direction of the town. There was pride in her voice as she continued. "Always the *doctor.*"

---

1. Hippocratic oath: credited to Hippocrates, (460?-377 B.C.) Greek physician called "the Father of Medicine" and administered to those entering the medical practice on receiving a degree after qualification.

AUTHOR'S NOTE

According to the information I gathered in Fort Worth, the sick man was Hayden Paul Lindrick and, as a result of Doc Leroy's skillful ministrations, he recovered from the burst appendix. Furthermore, backed by Doc and Waco, he brought a peaceful and satisfactory conclusion to the right-of-way dispute. Doc also learned the truth about his parents' death.

After leaving Lampasas County, Lindrick had quit Texas. Finding himself employed under the assumed name "Haynes Parker Lashricker" as a trouble-shooter for the Union Pacific Railroad, he had contrived to carry out his duties without drawing attention to himself. Then he had been assigned to help build railways in Mexico and Central America. As his return to the United States coincided with the right-of-way dispute on the U.P.R.'s spur line to Kenton, he had gone there to take control and contain the trouble.

As the Colt Pocket Pistols had been a present from his mother, Lindrick had been disinclined to part with them. So, although he had realized they might offer a clue to his true identity, he had retained them and, when it became feasible, had them rechambered for metallic cartridges. They had been stolen by Blaby, but Lindrick had not sent Royster to retrieve them. Having learned where the young thief had gone, the hired gun had followed of his own initiative, hoping to earn "Lashricker's" approbation by returning with the highly prized weapons.

Finally, hearing that Doc was coming to Kenton and Waco had been asked to meet him, Lindrick had decided the time had come for him to learn the truth. So the invitation was made, but the burst appendix intervened. On his recovery, Lindrick and Doc had become good friends. Having helped to bring the right-of-way dispute to an end, the young Texan had returned to Two Forks. There, until he died, he was in practice and was known to everybody in Utah as DOC LEROY, M.D.